"Being on top is bette

MID-CONTINENT PUBLIC LIBRARY - INT
15616 E. 24 HWY.
INDEPENDENCE, MO 64050

3 0007 13444035 2

bottom..."

"Not always." Hailey's wor
The look in her eyes was hot, sexy.

"Being on top has a few definite benefits," Gage
murmured, now having completely switched places
so her back was against the wall and his toward the
ballroom.

"Does it? Like wh
they were lost i
white fur brim c

D1401544

Need, stronger
flirtation, surged through Gage. He angled his body
so Hailey was trapped between him and the wall.

For a second, one delicious second, he just stared.
The tempting display of luscious flesh, mounded
above the tight satin binding her breasts.

The need intensified. Took on a sharp, hungry edge.

"Like this," he said, giving in to its demand. He took
her mouth, intending to be gentle.

But the kiss was carnal and raw and dancing on the
edges of desperate. Tongues tangled. Lips slid, hot
and wet.

And she tasted just as sweet

Mid Continent Public Library
15616 E US HWY 24
Independence, MO 64050

But the sounds she made we

WITHDRAWN
FROM THE RECORDS OF THE
MID-CONTINENT PUBLIC LIBRARY

Dear Reader,

I love the holidays, with all of the festivity they bring. But I have to admit, I've never actually attended a Christmas party that required costumes. Doesn't that sound fun? Would you go like Hailey, as a cute holiday icon? Or like Gage, as a beloved story character? Me? I think I want to be the Sugarplum Fairy. Flitting from dreamer to dreamer, sprinkling happy thoughts and holiday wishes sounds pretty awesome.

I love Hailey, and was so happy to write her journey not only to love, but to finding that inner strength she always had but never seemed to trust herself to use. She was fun to spend time with, because she's one of those girls who, even though she worries about being bad, she has no problem being naughty. Which was a great contrast to Gage, who is sure he's bad, but discovers he's a lot nicer inside than he's comfortable with. Together, they figure out a way to balance their ambitions, their personalities and their future.

I hope you enjoy curling up with *Naughty Christmas Nights*. I also hope you have a fabulous holiday season, filled with happy wishes, sweet treats and nice surprises!

Happy reading,

Tawny Weber

USA TODAY Bestselling Author

Tawny Weber

——

Naughty Christmas Nights

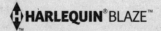
HARLEQUIN® BLAZE™

If you purchased this book without a cover you should be aware
that this book is stolen property. It was reported as "unsold and
destroyed" to the publisher, and neither the author nor the
publisher has received any payment for this "stripped book."

Recycling programs
for this product may
not exist in your area.

ISBN-13: 978-0-373-79782-0

NAUGHTY CHRISTMAS NIGHTS

Copyright © 2013 by Tawny Weber

All rights reserved. Except for use in any review, the reproduction or
utilization of this work in whole or in part in any form by any electronic,
mechanical or other means, now known or hereafter invented, including
xerography, photocopying and recording, or in any information storage
or retrieval system, is forbidden without the written permission of the
publisher, Harlequin Enterprises Limited, 225 Duncan Mill Road,
Don Mills, Ontario, Canada M3B 3K9.

This is a work of fiction. Names, characters, places and incidents are
either the product of the author's imagination or are used fictitiously,
and any resemblance to actual persons, living or dead, business
establishments, events or locales is entirely coincidental.

This edition published by arrangement with Harlequin Books S.A.

For questions and comments about the quality of this book,
please contact us at CustomerService@Harlequin.com.

® and TM are trademarks of Harlequin Enterprises Limited or its
corporate affiliates. Trademarks indicated with ® are registered in the
United States Patent and Trademark Office, the Canadian Trade Marks
Office and in other countries.

Printed in U.S.A.

ABOUT THE AUTHOR

USA TODAY bestselling author Tawny Weber has been writing sassy, sexy romances since her first Harlequin Blaze was published in 2007. A fan of Johnny Depp, cupcakes and color coordination, she spends a lot of her time shopping for cute shoes, scrapbooking and hanging out on Facebook.

Readers can check out Tawny's books at her website, www.TawnyWeber.com. There, they can also join her Red Hot Readers Club for goodies like free reads, chapter excerpts, recipes, contests and much more.

Books by Tawny Weber

To browse a current listing of all Tawny's titles, please visit www.Harlequin.com.

To my awesome brothers, Ron and Kevin!
I love you guys.

Prologue

HOLIDAYS SUCKED.

Gage Milano had no issue with the *idea* of a holiday. Celebrations were great. Kinda like parties, which he rocked. Or remembering and commemorating events, which showed respect. Gage was all for respect.

But holidays?

Holidays meant family.

Obligation.

That freaking heritage crap.

Gage looked up from his plate. Crystal glinted, china gleamed. Ornate flower arrangements in fall tones lined the center of the rosewood table big enough to seat two dozen people. Which was twenty-one more than were sitting here now.

Stupid.

There was a perfectly sized, comfortable table in the breakfast room. But no. Couldn't eat Thanksgiving dinner in the breakfast room. Not because it wasn't fancy enough. Nope. Gage figured it was because his father was still trying to drive home the fact that in the Milano dynasty, he still had the biggest…table.

Marcus Milano was all about who was biggest. Best. Holding the most control. Something he loved, probably more than his sons. He'd taught Gage and Devon to be fierce competitors. From playing T-ball to pitching deals, he'd set the bar high and dared both his sons to accept nothing but a win. Unfortunately, with two of them, that meant one of them was always losing. Something Marcus always found a way to capitalize on.

As if hearing Gage's thoughts and ready to prove them right, Marcus looked up from his perfectly sliced turkey and portion-controlled serving of carbs to bellow down the table.

"Gage. New venture for you to take on."

Ahh, dinnertime demands. The Milano version of conversation.

"No room." Gage scooped up a forkful of chestnut dressing and shot his father a cool smile. "I'm in meetings with my own clients next week, then I'm on vacation."

"Make room," Marcus barked. "I want this account."

Ahh, the joys of being under the cozy family umbrella. Gage might be thirty years old, have a rep as a marketing genius, be the VP of a Fortune 500 company and own his own marketing start-up, which was quickly racking up enough success that he'd be forced to make some decisions soon.

But in his father's mind he was still at the old man's beck and call. There to do the guy's bidding.

It wasn't that Gage didn't appreciate the opportunities Milano had afforded him. But dammit, the company's success was as much because of him as anyone else. When he and Devon had come on board six years previous, it'd been sinking under the economic collapse. Between Devon's restructuring and Gage's marketing, they'd turned it around.

The old guy didn't see it that way, though. To him, he was Milano and his sons simply adjuncts.

Gage glared down the table. Pointless, since his father was nearsighted and too far away to notice. Not that he'd care if he could. Marcus Milano had built his rep on not giving a damn. So Gage shifted his anger across the table at his brother.

Devon, his black hair and blue eyes the spitting image of their father, only grinned.

"You're the king of the sales pitch, little brother. You know how we depend on you for these special projects."

Devon was also the king of bullshit.

"I don't have time," Gage repeated, his words delivered through the teeth of his own smile. "I've been going full speed ahead for six quarters with no break. When I signed that multimillion-dollar deal last month for the electronics division, we all agreed I was off the books until the end of the year."

Five weeks away from Milano. Time to chill, to relax. Hightail it to the Caribbean, where he could lie on the beach, chug the booze and check out the babes. And think.

Think about his future.

Think about leaving Milano.

Weigh the risks of going out on his own.

The old man had built a multipronged business with its fingers in various consumer pies. Milano made everything from tech to textiles. Devon was R & D, Research & Development. He came up with the ideas, put together whatever new product he thought would reel in more coin for the very full Milano coffers.

Gage was marketing. He could sell anything. Water to a drowning man. Silicone to a centerfold. Reality to the paranoid.

He knew people. What made them tick, what turned them on.

A trait that served him well, in business and in pleasure.

A trait that told him that getting away from this dinnertime trap was going to be one helluva feat.

"Off the books except in an emergency," Marcus said

around his mouthful of oyster stuffing. "This is an emergency."

"An emergency is pictures of Devon doing a donkey being displayed on the cover of *People* magazine. An emergency is the accounting department being caught using our computer system to embezzle from a foreign government or your last wife showing up pregnant, claiming the baby is yours. Whatever new product you want to peddle isn't a marketing emergency."

"I say it is."

Gage ground his teeth. Before he could snap, his brother caught his eye.

"Look, it's an easy deal," Devon said quietly, forking up a slice of turkey and swirling it through his buttery puddle of potatoes. "We're launching that lingerie line. The merchandise is ready. We just need a platform. Marketing came up with a great idea."

"Then why do you need me?"

"You know Rudolph department stores?"

"Dirty old man with the Midas touch and a handful of elite stores in California and New York?"

"That's the one. His spring fashion launch is an exclusive deal guaranteed to put any line he includes on the map. He's never missed. Whether it's because he has a keen eye or because the fashion industry is a bunch of lemmings, waiting for him to call the next trend, I don't know. But if we get that lingerie contract, Milano is gold in the fashion field."

Gage shook his head. He was a marketing consultant. He specialized in consumer branding, digital management and online strategic development. Nothing in that description said anything about talking to eccentric billionaires about women's underwear.

"Seriously, it's not going to take up more than a few days of your time. Rudolph is announcing his choices next weekend, and the contract will be signed and delivered before Christmas. You go in, make the deal and leave." Before Gage could point out that anyone could go in and pitch this, Devon dropped his voice even lower and added, "You can even add the time you lose on this to the New Year. You'll still get your five weeks off."

"This isn't about the time off." Even though that was a part of it. "It's about respecting our agreement."

"Look, I've had to set aside my projects to take on this new online store the old man wants to launch. It's not going to kill you to hit the beach a few days—or even a week— later than you'd planned."

So that was it. Lifting his pilsner glass, Gage gave his brother a dark look. Someday, one of them was going to be at the helm of Milano. The question was, which one? Marcus had made it clear that to run the company, his sons had to do three things: Be absolutely loyal. Prove they were more worthy than the other. And not piss him off.

Gage and Devon had realized a few years back that it was going to take building their own business success separate from Milano to prove their worth. The trick, of course, was doing that while not jeopardizing rules one and three. And more important, doing it faster and better than the other brother.

Or in Devon's case, while sabotaging the other brother's chances of doing it first.

"You're playing dirty," Gage said decidedly.

"I'm playing to win."

"What're you two muttering about down there?"

"We're talking about our tradition of breaking the wish-bone," Gage shot back, not taking his eyes off Devon. "I'm thinking we should sweeten the pot. In addition to the 10K for the winner, I think the loser can take on this new project of yours."

Devon's grin slipped. He couldn't talk his way around a

wishbone bet. There were no cards to slip out of his cuffs. It was a straight-on deal with lady luck. And of the two of them, Gage always had better luck with the ladies.

"Fine. You win, I take the deal. But if I win, I get to pick your costume for the Christmas party this deal requires you to attend."

Gage grimaced.

A Christmas costume party? What the hell kind of joke was this?

Appetite gone, he shoved his plate away.

Yeah. He hated the holidays.

1

HAILEY NORTH LOVED the holidays.

All the glitter and fun. Smiling faces glowing with joy, the secrets and excitement. And the gifts. Gifts and surprises always rocked. Especially hard-earned ones, presented at a fancy dress-up ball. Or, in this case, a ballroom packed with the rich and influential of the Northern California fashion scene all dressed up like holiday cartoons.

She should be ecstatic. Over-the-moon excited.

Tonight she'd finally be sure that her lingerie company wouldn't be joining Father Time in waving goodbye at the end of the year.

Instead, she was afraid the past couple of months of financial worries and stress over keeping her company had sent her over the edge into Crazyville.

Here she was surrounded by male models and wealthy designers, many of the most gorgeous specimens of the opposite sex to be found in the Bay Area. And it was the six-and-a-half feet of green fur, snowshoes and a bowling-pin shaped body across the room that was making her hot.

Hailey squinted just to be sure.

Nope. There was absolutely nothing enticing about the costumed guy at the bar. But sex appeal radiated off him like a tractor beam, pulling her in. Turning her on.

Green fur, for crying out loud.

Wow. Month after month of no sex really did a number on a healthy woman's libido.

Or maybe it was a year dedicated to the objective of making romance sexy. Of studying romantic fantasies, and finding ways to tastefully re-create them in lingerie form and show women that as long as they felt sexy, they were sexy.

Or, possibly, it might have something to do with the glass of champagne she'd knocked back for a little social courage when she'd walked into a ballroom filled with high-powered movers and shakers, most of whom had more money in their wallets than she had in her bank account. And all of them here to impress Rudy Rudolph, a department-store tycoon with a wicked sense of fun and prized openings in his new spring fashion lineup.

She glanced at her empty champagne flute, then at the bar. She should trade this in for something nonalcoholic. Something that didn't make her go tingly over green, grouchy holiday figures.

Then the Grinch pushed back his fur to check the time. When the hairs on his fingers caught on his leather watch-band, he yanked off the gloves in an impatient move, tossing them on the bar.

Thirst forgotten, Hailey stared at his hand as he reached for his own drink. Long and lean, with tapered fingers. Even from across the room, his palm looked broad. Her mind played through every hand-to-penis-size euphemism she'd ever heard and came up with the only conclusion possible.

The Grinch was hung.

The only question was, did he go for cute elves? Or was he strictly a man-and-his-dog kind of guy? Maybe she should have dressed up like a Who?

She'd taken two steps toward him, her body desperate to find out, before she caught herself.

No. She was here for business.

She peered at the baggy, saggy, furry back and grimaced. Not for fun. No matter how big the fun's hands
were.

"Hailey, darling."

Relieved, both at the distraction from lusting after the
Grinch and at there actually being someone here who knew
her name, Hailey turned.

Her social smile shifted to genuine delight at the sight
of the man who'd made this night possible for her. Jared
Jones, assistant to the wealthiest—and most eccentric—
tycoon in the department-store business.

Jared had taken her under his wing last summer when
they'd met in an elevator. Hailey had been on her way to
pitch her lingerie designs to the sales team and Jared had
been bemoaning a rip in his shirt. Before they'd reached
the sixth floor, she'd pulled out some fabric tape for a
temporary mend, earning his gratitude and his endless
devotion.

Apparently, a fashion faux pas was, to some, the end
of the world.

"Jared," she greeted, leaning in for a hug but careful not
to let him bump her head. It'd taken her twenty minutes
to get the bell-festooned elf hat pinned to her curls in a
way that didn't make her hair look like fluffy poodle ears.

"I love your gingerbread-man costume. Is that your favorite holiday character?" she asked, flicking her finger
on one of his cheerful, oversize buttons. Her eyes widened
before she laughed aloud as she noted the words *Eat Me*
etched on the red plastic.

"Edible goodness, that's me," he said with a wink. Then
he shifted his head to the left and gave a little wag of his
chin. "And if all goes well, that drummer boy over there
will be having a taste before the night is out."

Used to Jared's aggressive sexuality by now, Hailey

gave the drummer an obligatory once-over before sharing an impressed look with her horny gingerbread friend.

"But look at you," he gushed, his loud enthusiasm aimed as much at getting the drummer's attention as it was appreciation for Hailey's costume. "You know, I've seen at least a dozen elves tonight, but you're the best by far. You look fabulous. Is everything you're wearing straight from your lingerie line?"

"Everything but the skirt," Hailey confirmed, arms wide as she gave a slow turn to show off the goods. Her candy-cane-striped bustier with its red satin trim and white laces paired nicely with her red stockings and their white seams up the back that ended in clever bows just below the hem of her green tulle ballerina skirt. She was proof positive that the right lingerie could make any woman feel sexy.

Nothing like a year in the gym, a carb-elimination diet and a great tan to make a girl look damned hot in lingerie.

Too bad she'd only hit the gym maybe four times in the past twelve months, loved carbs like she loved her momma and was closer to winter-white than sun-kissed tan.

But that was the beauty of Merry Widow lingerie. A girl didn't have to have a supermodel body to look—and feel—fabulous in it.

"Oh, darling," Jared breathed in admiration as he completed his inspection.

Hailey didn't have to follow his gaze to know where he was staring. After all, the guy might not be interested in what her lingerie was covering, but he was all about fashion.

And her boots were pure fashion candy.

The white Manolo booties were an early Christmas present from her father. Well, not really *from* him, since he never knew what to get her. But she'd bought them last month with the holiday check he'd sent, so that made them his gift to her.

"Hailey, you have the best taste in footwear," he sighed. "Those boots are perfect. And such a great touch to bring the outfit from cute to couture."

"Thanks. Will Mr. Rudolph be arriving soon?" she asked, shifting from one foot to the other. She wiggled her toes in her most excellent boots as a reminder that a girl could handle anything if she was wearing fabulous footwear. "Since he's announcing his choices for the spring exclusives, shouldn't he do it before all the designers are drunk?"

While she was still tipsy enough to use getting one of those prized exclusives as an excuse to seduce the Grinch.

"Drunk designers only add to Rudy's sense of fun," Jared told her with a sly grin. He didn't say a word about the contracts, though. She knew he knew who'd been chosen. And he knew she knew. But they both knew she wouldn't ask.

"Quit obsessing," Jared said, giving her a nudge with his shoulder and leaving a streak of glitter on her arm.

"Maybe you should see if the drummer boy's sticks are worth checking out." She tilted her head toward the guy he'd been scoping. "I can't clear my head enough to be fun company."

"Darling, I'm here to enjoy the party with my favorite designer. If there was anything I could do to set your mind at ease so you could give the party the appreciation it deserves, I would. But you know me—I don't kiss and tell."

Giving in to her nerves, and reminding herself that she'd taken a cab here, Hailey traded her empty champagne glass for a full one, then arched one brow at Jared.

"Okay. So I don't spill company secrets." He hesitated, then wrinkled his nose and leaned closer. "At least not the ones that could get me fired."

Then he looked past her again. This time when his face

shifted, it wasn't into lustfully suggestive lines. Instead, he came to attention.

"I don't think the news will be secret for long, though," he told her, twirling his finger to indicate she turn herself around.

"Welcome, welcome."

Hailey, along with the rest of the ballroom, turned around and came to the same subtle attention that Jared had as a skinny Santa took the stage with two helpers dressed in swaths of white fur and a whole lot of skin.

She leaned forward, peering at the trio. The nerves in her stomach stopped jumping for a few seconds as she stared in shock. "Wow. Mr. Rudolph sure looks different without his tie."

Or maybe it was the fact that the pervy old guy was shirtless under his plush red jacket. Wasn't he in his seventies? Now, that wasn't a pretty sight. Afraid to look at it too long, in case it rendered her blind, Hailey glanced at the rest of the crowd. Nobody else seemed surprised.

"Thank you, everyone," he said, "for joining the Rudolph-department-store annual holiday costume party. As you can see, my favorite character is Santa Claus. Appropriate since I'm the man giving out the gifts tonight."

Fingernails digging into the soft flesh of her palms, Hailey puffed out a breath, trying to diffuse the nerves that'd suddenly clamped onto her intestines.

This was it. The big announcement.

She felt like throwing up.

"This year, instead of simply awarding spring women's-line contracts, I've decided to make things fun. I've chosen two favorite designers in each department. Women's wear, shoes and lingerie. Those designers will compete through the holiday season for the top spot."

Hailey's stomach fell. Competing? That didn't sound good. She wasn't the only one who thought so, either, if the muttering and hisses circling the room were anything to go by.

She gave Jared a puzzled look, trying to shrug off the sudden despair that gripped her. The contracts weren't being awarded tonight? But she needed to know. Without that contract, she was going to lose her business.

Jared ignored her stare, tilting his head pointedly to get her to pay attention.

She dragged her gaze to the stage with a frown. Instead of looking abashed, the old man seemed delighted by the angry buzz. His grin shifted from wicked to a visual cackle as he held up one hand for silence.

It took all of three seconds for him to be obeyed.

"So without further ado, here are the finalists in women's wear," he announced. A model featuring an outfit from each line crossed the stage behind him as he named the designer.

Hailey swallowed hard, trying to get past the tight worry in her throat. It wasn't as if she'd irresponsibly put all of her hopes on this deal. It was more a matter of everything else falling apart until this deal was all that was left to hope for.

She shifted from one foot to the other, trying to appreciate the gorgeous shoes as Rudolph announced the designer finalists for footwear. But not even the studded black leather stilettos could distract her worry.

Then he got to lingerie.

She didn't even listen to the names.

She just watched the models, her eyes locked with desperate hope on the curtain they entered from.

One strutted out in a wickedly sexual invitation in leather. It was the complete opposite of the Merry Widow's style, a look that screamed sex. Hot, kinky sex.

Hailey frowned. It wasn't her style, of course. But it was appealing. *If you like hot, kinky sex.*

Did she like hot, kinky sex? She'd never had the opportunity to find out. For a second, she wondered if the Grinch was into leather. Before she could imagine that, worry crowded the sexy thoughts right back out of her brain. She held her breath.

"And last but not least, Merry Widow Lingerie." Echoing the announcement was a model in a white satin chemise trimmed in tiny pink rosebuds, a design Hailey had labeled Sweet Seduction.

Fireworks exploded in her head, all bright lights, loud booms and overwhelming excitement.

"Ohmygod, ohmygod, ohmygod," she chanted, hopping up and down in her gorgeous booties. She spun around to grab Jared in a tight hug, then did another little dance. "That's me. That's me. I made it."

She made it. She had a chance.

An hour later, she was still giddy. It wasn't a contract, but it wasn't a rejection, either. And she'd learned young to take what she could get.

"This is so cool." Ever since Santa Rudolph's announcement, people kept coming up to congratulate her. That part was great. What was even better, though, were the compliments about her designs, which were displayed all around the room.

She felt like a rock star.

"I'm excited for you, darling. I am sorry it's not a definitive answer, though," Jared said quietly, his face taking on a rare seriousness. "I know how bad you need this deal, and I've been pitching hard for you. But Rudy got this wild notion that a contest would bring in more publicity and make it more fun. He'll decide before the New Year, though. He has to for marketing purposes."

"What kind of publicity?" Big publicity? Good publicity? Could it net her some new clients, maybe a few features in the fashion rags? Hailey's stomach danced again.

"Well…" Jared drew out, wrinkling his glittery nose. "I

honestly don't think he has a lot of publicity lined up. We were all under the impression that he was simply choosing a single designer for each line. But Friday he talked to some marketing guru who convinced him that it'd bring in great promotion if he made it a competition of some sort instead of a straight-up announcement."

"Who makes the final decision?" she wondered.

Jared pulled another face and shrugged. Clearly he didn't like not being in the know any more than she didn't like not having a clue.

But before Hailey could ask more questions, they were joined by a dapper-looking guy dressed like a festive reindeer with his green-and-red-plaid bow tie.

"Congratulations, Ms. North. I'm Trent Lane, the photographer for Rudolph department stores. I was happy to see your designs in the running. I've taken test shots of each submission and yours is my favorite."

"Really?"

"Really. It seems to epitomize romance. But sexy romance. The boudoir-photo kind, not the *Hustler*-spread kind."

Hailey giggled, wondering if the leather getups were *Hustler* material.

"It's my favorite, too," Jared agreed. "I told you when I first saw the line. It's perfect. Next season is all about nostalgia with overtones of passion. Bridal fresh but womanly confident."

Hailey wrinkled her nose, wondering if he realized he'd just described her gorgeous designs in the same terms used for feminine-hygiene products.

"Baby's breath and air ferns lining the runway. Satin backdrops. Maybe one of those long couch things, like Cleopatra would lounge on," Trent mused, falling into what she immediately saw was a creative brainstorming habit between him and Jared.

"A chaise. Perfect," Jared agreed. Tapping his chin, he added, "Maybe carried down the runway by four muscle-bound sex slaves?"

"That's not romantic," Trent dismissed. "You know Rudy really wants to lead the trend this season. If you suggest sex slaves, he might seriously consider Cassia Carver's mesh love sleeves for a part of the women's-wear line."

Hailey barely kept from shuddering. Avant-garde minis and maxis made up most of Cassia's line, and while they were edgy and fun, they would hardly compliment Merry Widow's lingerie. They would, she realized with a frown, go great with Milano's leather.

Suddenly the simple contract she'd thought she'd have was now even more complicated. All of the choices were going to have to flow together into a single, cohesive spring debut.

"Even if Rudy wants mesh and love slaves, there's no way marketing will go for it," Jared dismissed. "They'd bury him in the horrible sales data from the last time mesh hit the runway."

Oh, yay. A point in her favor. She just had to make sure she racked enough to win this baby. Hailey held her breath, willing herself to look invisible. Maybe if the two men forgot she was there, they'd spill some insider info that she could mop up and use.

"Well, Rudy wants Cherry Bella to model the entire spring line, and Merry Widow will look perfect on her."

Hailey couldn't contain her little *eep* of excitement.

Her designs? Perfect? Cherry Bella?

Oh, man. That shooting star was getting close enough that she could almost feel the heat.

"She'd look great in Merry Widow or Milano's," Trent agreed. "It's really going to come down to whichever line Cherry wants to wear. She'll be the final judge of all the lines, I'm guessing."

"Rudy has to get her signed first. And so far, she's not interested."

Trent looked to the left. Jared and Hailey looked, too. Then he looked to the right. They obediently followed his gaze. Forgetting that she was supposed to be invisible, Hailey leaned in just as close as Jared did to listen.

"I hear Rudy's pulling out all the stops. He's crazy to get Cherry signed. He's tried everything. Promised her the moon. So far, no go. He's shifted all his promises to her agent now." Trent gave them both a wide-eyed look, then nodded sagely, his reindeer ears bobbing in emphasis. "Whoever gets him Cherry Bella? They're golden."

Excitement ran so fast through Hailey's body, she shivered with it. Her lingerie was perfect for Cherry. The statuesque redhead had started as a soulful torch singer, but lately had branched into modeling and a few minor acting gigs, as well. Merry Widow's flowing, feminine designs would suit her as though they'd been custom made.

All Hailey had to do was cinch the deal.

She'd find Cherry's agent, charm him or her into listening to a personal pitch on how perfect Merry Widow designs would look on the retro singer.

"Do the other designers know?" she wondered aloud. Seeing the guys' arch expressions, she scrunched her nose and gave a shrug. What? They all knew she wasn't really invisible. "Just wondering."

"It's pretty hush-hush since a lot of competitors are always big to get a jump on Rudolph's spring debuts. So unless the other designers are chatting up Rudy's staff, I doubt they have a clue."

Jared's snort of laughter was more sarcastic than amused.

"Which means no," he explained at Hailey's questioning look, a little of the sugary glitter flaking off his face as he sneered. "Your competitors are all well established, with top-of-the-line reps, darling. They, unlike you, have huge egos. None of them see the need to fraternize with the help. They talk to Rudy, or they don't talk at all."

She peered through the costumed crowd, looking for any of the lingerie-clad models circling the room. She sighed as one lithe blonde floated by in a Merry Widow nightie. Cotton flowed. Lace rippled. The pearl buttons down the front caught the light, even as the delicate fabric molded to the woman's perfect body.

So romantic.

And so perfect for the Rudolph account, especially if he got Cherry as his spokesmodel.

She didn't want to jinx it but the little voice in her head was already planning the victory-dance moves.

"I'm surprised Cherry's agent isn't all over this deal," Hailey mused, wondering what they were holding out for. "A contract with Rudolph department stores would rocket her from national to international exposure, wouldn't it?"

"Oh, yeah," Jared agreed, looking like a dejected gingerbread boy with his furrowed brow. "We can't figure out what the problem is. Rudy'd be tearing his hair out if he wasn't already bald."

"Best we can figure, it's because the agency is one of those co-op places. The agents all work together on every client. Make decisions by consensus. We don't even know which agent is at the party. Guy, gal, nobody's got a clue," Trent complained, looking like a very grumpy reindeer whose gossip rations were being withheld. "Like I said, whoever reels her in is going to be golden."

Then a passing model dressed in a fishnet candy cane and spangles shaped like question marks caught his eye. He straightened his bow tie, gave Jared and Hailey an absent smile, then tilted his head. "Well, I think I'll go talk up the models and see if any of them are repped by the same agency as Cherry."

With that, and a leering sort of grin, he was gone.

"So what do you think? Do I have a shot?" Hailey asked as soon as he left. Her gaze flew around the room as if the infamous agent might have hung a neon sign around his or her neck, just for fun. If she could find the agent, she could pitch her own designs for Cherry. If she could get the agent enthused, she'd have an inside track. Maybe even a guaranteed deal.

Excitement bubbling, Hailey gave the room another searching look. Her gaze landed on Trent, who'd apparently given up on seducing the woman in mesh and was now talking to the sexy Grinch.

Her excitement took on a totally different edge at the sight of that Grinchy butt. The hood of the costume now pushed back, she could see his hair, so black it reflected the blue and white Christmas lights of the tree next to him, wave into the green fur of his collar.

Her nipples tingled against the tight satin layers of her bustier. Her thighs turned to mush, only the sheer red silk of her stockings holding them together.

Oh, yeah. He was definitely the hot, kinky, sexy type of guy.

All she had to do was look at him and she was more excited than she'd been with any of the lovers she'd ever had. Or even all of them, combined.

And all she was gazing at was the back of his head. That was better than being turned on by his furry back, wasn't it?

Her breath a little on the shallow side, she sighed and wondered how great it'd be to strip that ugly fur off and see what kind of body was beneath the costume. Could it be as sexy as she was imagining? Long and lean, with strong thighs and washboard abs? Shoulders she could cling to as she rode him like a wild stallion?

She'd just flown a few miles closer to catching her

shooting star. Didn't she deserve a treat? Could she do it? Go talk to him? Ask his opinions on hot, kinky sex. Leather or lace. Roses or studs.

Her face, throat and chest all on fire now, either with lust or embarrassment, Hailey quickly drank the rest of her champagne and exchanged the glass with a passing waiter, hoping the bubbles would cool the fire blazing in her belly.

"Hailey, darling? Where'd you go? I've been filling you in on all of the Rudolph stores' holiday plans and you haven't said a word. What's got you so distracted?"

Unwilling to admit the horrifying truth, that she was all hot and horny for a guy whom she'd only seen from the side and back, both of which were covered in puke-green fur, Hailey tore her gaze away and gave Jared an apologetic look.

"Nothing. Just, you know, wondering if that guy Trent's talking to might be Cherry's agent," she improvised.

Almost on tiptoes to see around the crowd, Jared peered in the direction of the bar. Then he gave a shrug.

"No clue." He looked again, this time giving a little hum of appreciation. His eyes were as wide as the buttons on the front of his gingerbread suit as he fanned one hand in front of his face. "I'll be happy to go find out, though."

She looked over again herself, wondering what had got his attention.

And almost fell to the floor, thanks to her weak knees.

Oh, baby.

The Grinch was gorgeous.

Her lust cells stood up and did a victory dance, vindicated in their attraction.

Her brain couldn't argue.

Because the man was definitely lust-worthy.

Raven-black hair swept back from his forehead in soft waves, framing a face that would make Michelangelo weep. Sharp planes, strong lines and intense brows were balanced by full lips and wide eyes. Even though she couldn't tell the color, she was sure those were the most gorgeous eyes she'd ever seen.

For the first time in forever, Hailey didn't know what she wanted more.

Success? Or the man across the room.

2

"THIS IS THE most ridiculous idiocy I've ever seen," Gage said decidedly, his glare spread equally across the ballroom at his cousin and at those butt-ugly green fur gloves he'd been forced to wear to this stupid party. "And what's with the babysitting duty, Trent? You lose a bet yourself?"

"More like blackmail," Trent muttered, watching yet another leggy blonde slink by with a regretful sigh. "Believe me, if I had a choice, I'd be long gone by now."

"Yeah? Well, so would I."

Once, a party like this would have appealed to Gage.

A bachelor's playground, complete with booze, babes and enough variety in the guest list to stave off boredom.

The requirement to dress like your favorite holiday character, though? That was where it all tipped right on over to idiocy.

Yet, here he was. Smothered in freaking fur. Didn't matter that it was almost December. San Francisco didn't get cold enough to make this costume anything but miserable.

"How'd they con you into this?" Trent asked, craning his head to one side to watch a woman's leather-clad ass as she worked the crowd. Gage vaguely recognized it. The leather, not the ass. It was one of the new Milano designs. Sexy Biker Babe, Devon had called it. Stupid, really. It looked hot, and definitely sent a strong sexual message. But who wore leather lingerie?

He gave an absent scan of the room, measuring the crowd, the reactions. There were enough people eyeing the leather with an appreciative look, as opposed to the ones peering in confusion at the mesh dresses some models were suffering in.

The most admiration seemed to be for the lacy getups floating through the room, though. The kind of lace you'd see on a forties pinup model, rather than the kind you'd see on a favorite internet porn site. Classy, he supposed it'd be called.

Noticing his attention, a tall brunette in a tasteful teddy and floor-length robe in white satin with fluffy trim gave him an inviting look before she stopped to exchange comments with a guest. The model moved on.

But Gage's gaze was locked on the woman she'd spoken with.

Helloo.

Interest stirred for the first time since he'd heard of this party, Gage straightened.

She was blonde and cute, with an air of sweetness surrounding her like a holiday promise. The women he usually went for were dark, sultry and cynical. So what was it about her that made him want to sit up and beg?

Sure, she was sexy. But even though her costume was obviously lingerie inspired, she was still stepping pretty close to the sedate line. His type usually danced on the edge of the slutty line.

Yet he wanted nothing more than to cross the room, toss her over his shoulder and haul her off to someplace where he could lick her wild. Obviously this work overload and insane costume were taking a toll on his sanity.

"Gage?"

"Huh?" With one last look to assure himself that she

wasn't his type, he yanked his attention back to his cousin. "What?"

"I said, how'd you get stuck with this gig? I thought you were on vacation."

"The old man played the emergency card, deeming getting the Rudolph contract to launch this new project top priority." He wasn't about to admit that he'd pulled the short end of a wishbone. A guy could only take so much humiliation at a time.

Used to his uncle's games, Trent didn't seem surprised.

"You do well enough on your own. And you hate working for your father. Why don't you just resign?"

Good question.

"It's not that easy. Nor is it something I want to talk about at a party full of people in their underwear and me in green fur."

Or anywhere else, for that matter.

Not because he was so private.

But because he really didn't know himself.

Money was a major factor. He'd seen plenty of successful people sink under the weight of running their own show.

Loyalty was another. He might hate the dictatorial way Marcus Milano ran things, but it was still a family company founded by his grandfather. As far back as he could remember, his father had claimed that Milano was run by Milanos. And Milanos were expected to make it a success. So much so that if one left, he was out. Out of the company, off the board and in the case of Gage's uncle when he'd quit, disinherited and ostracized by the family.

And there was always the competition between him and Devon. Gage glared at the furry gloves again, damned if he'd lose to his brother in an even bigger way. When he went out on his own his start-up would be bigger, stronger, more successful than any and all of Devon's put together.

None of which were thoughts he was particularly proud of.

The perfect distraction, the pretty blonde elf caught his eye again. Her eyes were huge, so big they dominated her face. A cross between adorable and arousing, with full lips and round cheekbones both a glossy red to match her stockings. Gage's gaze dropped again to those legs. They were very excellent legs, long and lean. The sheer red hose and sexy little boots reminded him of a candy cane. An image echoed by the striped bustier hugging breasts so sweet they almost overflowed the tight fabric.

Gage rocked back on his heels, humming in appreciation.

She didn't belong here.

Her costume might.

Her party partner might.

And the holiday theme might.

But she looked too sweet to be interested in something as lame as this event.

So sweet he wanted to invite her to a private party. One where he could taste her, just there where the satin met that soft flesh, and see if she was as tasty as she looked. Like a delicious Christmas treat.

"So, hey, I've got instructions from Devon I've gotta follow." Trent's uncomfortably muttered words pulled Gage's attention away from the sexy blonde.

"You babysat, you probably took pictures to share on Facebook, and you verified that I stayed until the announcement." Gage was still irritated that the best he'd been able to get out of this deal was to be in the competition for the contract. Despite his best pitch, Rudolph hadn't been willing to set aside his initial favorites. "I've done my part. I'm done. Showing up in this stupid costume was the end of my assignment."

"Yeah, sure. But, well, my instructions were to wait until after the announcement, and if Milano was in the running for the contract, to issue a new bet." Trent looked a little ill at this point.

Gage laughed so loud, half the room glanced their way.

"Is that reindeer headgear pressing too tight into your brain? You really think I'm going to take another one of Devon's bets?"

"C'mon. You know he'll make my life hell if I don't follow through," Trent beseeched, looking so pitiful even his antlers drooped. "It's not a big deal. I just have to mention that there's a bet on the table, and give you this."

This, Gage found out when Trent pulled it from the inner pocket of his Fruit-Stripe-gum-colored jacket, was an envelope. "That's it?" Gage asked, gesturing with his gloves to the paper. The envelope was thick and black, and he figured his brother had been trying for ominous. The guy was a little too dramatic.

"This is it," Trent agreed, holding the envelope closer. When Gage didn't take it, he set it on the bar with a shrug. "My instructions were simply to make sure you knew there was a bet and to make it available if you were interested."

"You did, and I'm not."

"No skin off my nose," Trent dismissed. Now that he was free, he was more focused on catching the eye of one of the mostly naked women than trying to change Gage's mind. "I'll let Devon know you met the terms of the bet. Oh, and can you tell him I did offer you the insider info? He promised to burn the pictures of… Well, it won't matter what they are of after tonight."

If Trent's grin was anything to go by, the evidence Devon had used to blackmail him was probably wearing a wedding ring. And just for handing over an envelope, that evidence was getting burned?

Gage frowned at the heavy black paper. His brother wasn't the type to let go of blackmail material that easily.

Always resourceful, Devon figured good dirt was worth using at least twice.

So whatever plan Devon was playing, it was big.

"Hold on," he said through his teeth, snatching up the envelope and ripping the heavy paper aside. He read the thick, purple papers quickly, shock seeping through his irritation. Then he read through them once more to be sure the itchy green fur hadn't impaired his comprehension.

No way in hell...

"He's willing to let me go?"

Trent leaned closer to read the letter, then gave a shrug. "Is that what it says? He told me to assure you that he's not bullshitting." Seeing Gage's doubtful look, Trent plastered on his most earnest expression. It went pretty well with the antlers and bow tie, actually. "He didn't give me details, just told me what to say if you opened the letter."

"What are you? His windup toy?"

"Funny you should mention toys. That's actually what those pictures..." Grimacing, Trent shook his head. "So, you gonna take the bet?"

Gage considered his options.

Being the trusting soul he was, Marcus Milano hadn't just used the threat that he'd cut them off if they ever left, he'd contractually tied his sons to Milano's.

But if Gage got this contract, his brother would arrange for an entire year of freedom. With full pay. Gage could do whatever he wanted, without losing his safety net or walking out on family obligations. In exchange, he just had to seal this lingerie deal.

"You gonna fill me in on what it'll take to win this Rudolph contract?"

"Why? You don't have any pictures of me, three blondes and a battery-operated rabbit."

All Gage did was shift. Just an inch. His shoulders back. His spine straighter. His chin lifted.

Then he arched one brow.

Trent's grin wilted.

"Look, I don't know anything. And what I do know is mostly rumor. But it's company rumor, so I can't tell. Your games with Devon aren't worth my job."

Unfazed, Gage nodded.

"I win this bet, I'll be gone for a year," he mused, taking a second to revel in that vision. A whole year, free of Milano. To travel without a tightly controlled, money-making itinerary. No board meetings, no R & D meetings, no personnel meetings. Just him and his own business.

He eyed his cousin. Yeah. He wanted that dream. Enough to take the bet and to bump the stakes.

"I'm gone a year," he repeated, "I got two choices. Garage my 'Vette. Or let someone play car-sitter."

"Your 'Vette?" Trent's eyes glazed over as if he was having a personal moment. Then he shook his head. "No way."

"Way."

It didn't take two seconds before his cousin grabbed his hand to seal the deal.

Everyone had a price.

Gage listened as Trent babbled on about a torch singer, a weird old man's trend obsession and secret agents.

"So whoever gets this singer to wear their line is gonna get the deal?" he confirmed.

Trent nodded. "If you get Cherry Bella to wear your lingerie line, you nail the contract."

And win the bet.

"And you're saying her agent is here, at the party, scoping it out to decide if any of the designs are worthy?"

"That's what I hear."

Gage's gaze shifted across the room again to the blonde. There was only one person here who didn't belong.

One very sexy, very tasty-looking person who seemed

out of place among the eccentric designers and the narcissistic models.

If he had to guess who the agent was, and apparently he did, he'd pick her.

And now that he'd picked her, he just had to charm her into choosing Milano for her client.

"Not a problem," he decided.

This was going to be quite the treat.

Beat his brother.

Win a year's freedom.

And make some time with a very sexy blonde.

Looked as if this party wasn't quite as idiotic as he'd thought.

HAILEY GULPED.

He was coming her way.

She'd lost count of how many glasses of champagne she'd had. Enough to make her head spin. But the tingling swirls going on right now had nothing to do with alcohol and everything to do with the Grinch.

The oh-so-deliciously-sexy Grinch.

"Trent looks like someone just gave him the keys to a houseful of horny women. I'm going to talk to him," Jared decided, clearly oblivious to Hailey's tingles, swirls or even her overheated cheeks. "I'll bet he figured out who the agent is."

"Go, go," Hailey encouraged with a little wave of her hand. She wasn't really shooing him away, so much as making room for the Grinch.

"Oh, baby," she sighed as he stopped next to her. He was even yummier up close and personal. A faint shadow darkened his chin, making her wonder if he was one of those guys blessed with a luxurious pelt of chest hair. She'd always wanted to get close enough to a guy like that so she could bury her face in the silky warmth and snuggle.

Her fingers itched to tug the zipper of his costume down and see for herself.

"Hello." The greeting was accompanied by a smile that, for all its charm, edged just this side of wicked.

His eyes were dark, so dark they seemed black in the party lights, with thick lashes and slashing brows. And they were staring at her with an intensity that made her want to check herself to make sure nothing had fallen out.

"Hi," she said, giving him a bright smile. At a delicate five-one, which was why the elf costume had been so inspired, she had to tilt her head back a little to see his face. Bells jingled. At first she wondered if that was a sign from Cupid. Then she remembered that it was Christmas, not Valentine's. And that she was wearing bells on her hat.

"I'm Gage," he murmured, taking her hand.

"Hailey," she said on a sigh as her fingers were engulfed by his. He was warm. Strong and gentle at the same time, and his skin felt so good she didn't want to pull away.

Her usual nerves at meeting a gorgeous, sexy man were nowhere to be found. Probably doing the backstroke through a river of champagne. But she wasn't drunk enough to do anything stupid, like unzip his costume with her lips right here in the middle of the ballroom.

After all, she didn't want hair between her teeth.

"What do you think of the party?" he asked, not taking those intense eyes off her as he tilted his head to indicate the room. It was as if he were looking past her cheerful smile and holiday bells into her soul, where he could peek at all of the secrets she hid there. Like her dreams. Her darkest, sexiest fantasies. And every single one of her fears.

That was both sexy as hell and the scariest thing she'd ever imagined.

"The party's great," she said, nerves starting to poke through the champagne bubbles. "I thought it was a fun theme, coming as your favorite holiday character. At least I did until I saw the guy dressed as a pair of Christmas balls waving his candy cane around."

The words echoed in Hailey's head as she realized what she'd said. Eyes wide with horror, she slapped her hand over her mouth. Not that she could take the words back, but maybe it'd help slow down the next stupid thing she tried to blurt out.

Gorgeous Gage the Grinch just laughed, though. A deep, full-bodied sound that eased her fear and made her grin right back. His gaze changed, softened, with his amusement. He was still sexy as all get-out, but now he seemed real. Not quite so much like a sexual fantasy sent to rip away all her inhibitions. More like an intriguingly attractive man who made her want to toss them away on her own.

"I guess I don't have to ask if you've been entertained by the various displays here this evening."

A movement across the room caught her eye. Hailey shifted her gaze, noting Jared, flanked by Trent and Mr. Rudolph, heading toward the door. He looked frantic, doing a subtle wave of his hand behind his boss's back and jerking his head around. Either he was trying to give her a message, or he was being hauled off against his will.

She tilted her head, trying to figure out what he was saying. Then she realized he was pointing at Gage and mouthing something. She gave a helpless shrug, totally clueless. His disgusted sigh came across loud and clear, though, then he held his hand to his ear, thumb and pinkie outstretched.

Call him.

Then, just as he was swept out the door by a jolly old man, he jabbed his fingers toward Trent.

"Looking for that pair of Christmas balls?" Gage teased.

"Oh, sorry," she said with an abashed grimace. "It's just

so distracting here. Like a circus, but instead of performing animals, it's a bizarre fashion statement, all wrapped
in holiday tinsel."

"And you're not into bizarre?"

Hailey arched her brow. Why did that sound as if he'd
just passed judgment and she'd somehow failed?

"Should I be?"

"Hardly. *Bizarre* generally means weird and confusing.
I'm not a fan of confusion."

"And the holidays?" she asked, gesturing to his costume. "Are they high on your list, or is your heart three
sizes too small?"

He opened his mouth, then shook his head and shut it
with a grin. "I'll skip over any size comparisons, if you
don't mind."

Delighted at his sense of humor, Hailey laughed.

"How about we leave size issues to my imagination
and skip right to the holiday question," she said with an
impish smile.

"Just as long as you have a good imagination."

"It's amazing."

"A lot of dreams?"

"Big ones," she assured him. "Huge, even."

He gave an appreciative grin, then at her arch look, it
faded to a deep, considering stare before he shifted his
gaze to the decorated trees and holiday props around the
room.

"I don't have a problem with the holidays, per se," he
admitted. The way he said it, slow and careful, as if he
were measuring each word, told her that he was a man
who valued honesty. He might dance around the truth. He
might refuse to answer. But whatever he did say, he expected to be held to it.

That kind of integrity was even sexier than his gorgeous

smile. Maybe not sexier than his body, but she couldn't say for sure since it was still covered in lumpy green fur.

"But there are parts you're not crazy about," she guessed, trying to stay on topic and quit undressing him with her mind. Especially now that her imagination was using the word *huge* in all its naked images.

"Sure. But you have to take the bad to get the good, right?"

No. She wanted to shake her head. The bad might show up from time to time, but the whole point was to avoid it if possible. To think positive and flow with the good.

But she wasn't sure her Pollyanna-esque argument was going to get very far with a guy who favored the Grinch.

"So which good parts are your favorite?"

"The food," he mused, gesturing to the Mrs. Claus walking by with a tray of sugar cookies. "Gotta love the desserts this time of year."

A man after her own heart.

"But as good as those cookies look, I'll bet you're sweeter. Like the candy cane your outfit reminds me of. But instead of peppermint, you'd be cherry flavored."

His words were low and flirtatious, his eyes dancing and hot as his gaze swept over her body as if he wanted to taste her and see.

Hailey swallowed hard. She knew she was totally out of her league. But she didn't care.

It was as if she were drowning in desire, passion burning low in her belly with a heat she didn't think anything could douse. She sure was ready to let him try, though.

Then his words washed over her like a lifeline, tugging at her attention.

What had he said?

Cherry?

A bright light went off in Hailey's head, clearing away the foggy fingers of passion. Ooh, she smiled as excitement pushed back—but didn't in any way extinguish—the hot desire in her belly.

Jared must have been trying to tell her that Gage was the agent. The man to persuade that her designs were perfect for his client.

Seriously?

Hailey almost laughed out loud.

First her designs were chosen as semifinalists.

Then the sexiest man she'd ever seen hit on her.

And now she had to do everything and anything in her power to make him crazy about her lingerie?

It was all Hailey could do to keep from clapping her hands together in delight.

This night rocked.

3

"So you don't seem like a designer or model," Hailey said, sliding a sideways glance at Gage. Not that all designers were, well, feminine. But the gorgeous man next to her was way too masculine, deliciously and temptingly masculine, for her to imagine him playing with ribbon and lace. Or even mesh and leather, unless they were exclusively in the bedroom.

His laugh echoed her assessment.

"Oh, no," he assured her. "I'm not a model. And I'm definitely not a designer."

And he didn't work for Rudolph's, or Jared would have told her. Which left, *dum da dum,* him being the agent.

Sweet. So sweet, she almost did her happy dance again.

"So you're clearly a fan of the holidays," he guessed, gesturing to her outfit. "And you look as if you're enjoying the party. Anything in particular impress you tonight?"

He had.

But she didn't think he was fishing for compliments.

Hailey tried to clear the champagne buzz from her head and pull together a strategy. She needed to pitch her heart out here. To make wow and impress him, not only with the designs themselves, but with her knowledge of the industry, of his client. And, because he was just so freaking yummy, maybe with herself.

It wasn't as if she was offering up her body in exchange for a good word to his client. More like she was willing to worship his body while never directly mentioning the client.

That wasn't stepping over any lines, was it?

"Hmm, there's so much to choose from," she mused as if her mind had retained anything other than impressions of him and the words *Get Cherry*. "I was really impressed with Rudolph's clever contest. The designs were all so diverse, weren't they?"

His eyes sharpened, as if she'd just triggered a switch. To what, she wasn't sure. But since he stepped closer, she hoped she could figure it out so she could trigger it at will.

"And your favorite?" he asked, so close she could feel his breath on her forehead. So close she could feel the warmth of his body wrapping around her.

She wanted to lean in and breathe deep. To snuggle in and nuzzle her nose in the curve of his shoulder. The tiny part of Hailey's brain that was still functioning at normal levels was trying to figure out what the hell was wrong with the rest of her. All she did was look at this guy and all of her senses were sucked into the lust cycle.

"Hailey?"

"Hmm?" She frowned, trying to remember what he'd asked.

"Do you have a favorite?"

"A favorite…?" Position? Flavor of body oil? Term for the male genitalia? "Oh, favorite designs?"

"Yeah. Are you drawn to any particular designer?"

There was that intense look again.

Hailey started to pitch her own line, then bit her lip. Maybe it was better to charm him first, before he realized she was one of the designers. That way, then she could gently lead him into the idea of Cherry and Merry Widow being the perfect match. She'd noticed one thing in this past year of trying to sell her wares—the minute someone thought you were pitching something, they went on the defensive.

Her gaze roamed over the masculine beauty of his face, making her sigh. Nope. She'd much rather he be receptive to anything she had to pitch.

So she shrugged instead and said, "There are a lot of great looks here tonight. I think it'd be fun to try to match each one to their perfect person." Hailey wanted to bounce in her Manolos, she was so proud of that subtle hint. Kinda like subliminal sales. She'd just lay a few bread crumbs here and there, and he could nibble his way to her line of thinking. "That's the key to a great design, isn't it? That it enhance the features, the personality, of the person wearing it."

"Do you really think there's someone that suits all of these, um, outfits?" he asked over the band, who'd turned their amps up louder now that people were hitting the dance floor. He gave a pair of sequined hot pants and a satin, cropped tee a doubtful look before arching a skeptical brow. Maybe because the outfit was the same nauseating green as his fur.

"I think everyone, and everything, has a perfect match," she said. Then she grimaced, worried her enthusiasm might be taken the wrong way—as if she were about to chase him down like a lovesick crazy woman who was looking for happy-ever-after forever promises. Instead of the right way, which was that they should get naked and see what happened when their bodies got sweaty together.

What'd happened to her? Hailey was almost as shocked at her body's reaction—instant horniness—as she was at her wild thoughts.

She rubbed one finger against her temple, as if she could reset her normal inhibition levels. She needed to stick with cheap champagne from now on. Clearly she couldn't handle the expensive stuff.

"What type of lingerie would match you perfectly?" he wondered aloud. His tone was teasing, but the look on his face made her stomach tumble as the lust spun fast, tangling with nerves.

To hell with resetting her inhibitions.

This was way more fun.

Her perfect match was a man who was there for her. Who wanted her for the long-term, not just for a convenient window of time. Perfect was fabulous sex, unquestioning support, faith in her abilities and enough love to want to actually dig in deep and be a part of her world, instead of flitting around the convenient edges.

But that was all someday thinking.

Tonight? Tonight perfect was dressed in green fur.

As if he heard her thoughts, the flirtatious heat faded from Gage's demeanor and his smile shifted from seductive to charmingly distant.

Hailey frowned as his look intensified, as if he were inspecting the far corners of her soul. The parts she kept hidden, even from herself.

Was he reading her mind when his eyes got all deep and penetrating like that? Did he know she was wondering if he was her match? Or was he the kind of guy who'd run, screaming with his furry tail between his legs, if he had a clue she was interested in more than business?

Before she could wonder too much about it, though, the floor show kicked off. All of the models hit the dance floor, "Gangnam Style." And Gage's attention shifted, so the heat in Hailey's belly had a chance to cool a little.

"Now, that's entertainment," he said with a laugh, wincing as more than one model had to grab her chest to keep it from flying out while dancing.

"It's getting wild," Hailey agreed, both amused and impressed at the same time. Wild or not, her designs looked great out there. Feminine and sexy. And it was nice to know her lingerie could dance horsey style.

"What do you say?" Gage asked, leaning in close so his words teased her ear. Hailey shivered, her nipples leaping to attention and her mind fogging again. "Want to get out of here?"

Despite her nipples' rapid agreement, Hailey hesitated.

She was willing to do a lot for her company. She was willing to do almost anything to get this contract. But while she was insanely attracted to Gage, she wasn't sure leaving with him was something she'd be proud of once the champagne cleared her system.

Correctly reading her hesitation, Gage gestured to the glass doors.

"How about a walk through the conservatory? It'll be quieter. We can talk, get away from the, um, dancing."

As if echoing his words, the music shifted to a raunchier beat. Hailey winced as the dancers shifted right along with it.

A walk. That was safe. They would still be in a fairly public arena and she'd be close enough to the party to remind herself that this was business. That should keep her from trying to rip that fur off Gage's body to see what was underneath.

"Sure," she agreed, accepting his invitation to tuck her arm into his. She tried to ignore the dance floor, where the hired help was doing a dance version of the upright doggy style. But she couldn't help blushing. Not because the moves were tacky. But because she wished she could do them, too. She couldn't, of course. Mostly because she was a lousy dancer.

She could—and should—get out of here before the dancers, and the champagne, gave her any more naughty ideas, though.

"A walk would be lovely."

GAGE WELCOMED THE cool night air like an alcoholic welcomed that first hit of gin. With greedy need and a silent groan of gratitude.

He'd been sweating like crazy in there.

Was it because of this god-awful hideous costume?

Or because of his body's reaction to the sweet, little elf next to him?

It had to be the costume.

Because he never sweated over women.

The lust wasn't a new thing. He'd spent most of his life surrounded by gorgeous women, so lust was as very familiar to him as breathing.

And it wasn't as if he had problems mixing business and pleasure. Gage worked with too many beautiful women to hamper himself with silly rules or false moral restrictions.

And while he wasn't a cocky ass, he'd had enough success with the ladies to feel both comfortable and confident that he could handle anything a woman had to offer.

Nope. He'd never had women problems.

So clearly, it must be the costume.

"Mr. Rudolph puts on quite a party," Hailey said as she wandered between marble columns wrapped in twinkling white lights. "Do you attend often?"

"This is my first," he admitted. "How about you?"

Gage didn't wander. Instead, he scoped the room, found a semisheltered wall and leaned against it. That way, she could come to him. She didn't, though. Instead, after an inscrutable look through those thick lashes, she shrugged and continued her slow meander through the conservatory.

"This is my first, too. I've talked to plenty of people who are involved behind the scenes, though. If the rumors are true, things are going to get pretty wild and naked in there soon."

Behind the scenes?

She must have a few models in there showing off the

wares. Theirs, and the designers. He debated how long to wait and steer the conversation toward some of her other clients. A minute or two, maybe. First he needed to figure her out. Usually by this point, fifteen minutes into their first meet, he'd completely pegged a person.

But Hailey the elf was a mystery.

"You don't sound disgusted by the idea of wild and naked," he observed.

Was she wilder than her sweet face and cute demeanor portrayed? His body stirred, very interested in finding out.

"Everyone has the right to enjoy the holidays in their own special way," she said, her laugh as light as the bells jingling on her hat. "And I like the idea that the lingerie samples might be so sexy, they inspire that kind of thinking."

"On the right woman, an elf hat and ballerina skirt inspires that kind of thinking," he murmured quietly.

Not so quietly that she didn't hear, if the pale pink washing over her cheeks was any indication. She didn't say anything, though. Just kept on wandering.

"So what did you find most interesting this evening?" she asked, trailing her fingers along the edge of a larger-than-life, white wicker sleigh filled with a tree, gifts and more lights. "Were you here for the shoes? There were some gorgeous new lines being shown. Or are you more a women's-wear kind of guy?"

Her arch smile was teasing and filled with as much light as the twinkling display around them. Gage had to wonder if she was always this cheerful or if she'd been hit with a little too much holiday cheer.

"I was only interested in the lingerie," he said, figuring it was time to start winding the conversation toward her coveted client. "At least I was until I saw you. Everything else sort of faded at that point."

"Uh-huh," she laughed. "Me versus a dozen perfect

women in lingerie. I can see how you were torn between the two views."

"Do you doubt me?"

At his mock offense, she stopped wandering and gave him a wide-eyed once-over. Then, finally, she joined him next to the nice, semiprivate wall.

"Doubt the Grinch? A figure known for his good cheer, holiday honesty and love of everything sweet and cuddly?"

Gage grinned. Damn, she was cute.

"Is that what he's for?" He looked down at the green fur monstrosity he was wearing and rolled his eyes. How appropriate. He had to hand it to his brother; the guy was clever with the inside jokes.

"You don't know? You're supposed to be portraying your favorite holiday character."

"I lost a bet."

"So you're not really all Grinchy about the holidays?" She tilted her head to one side as she asked the question, her bells tinkling as if to dare him to deny the joy of the season.

Gage hesitated. He never tried to hide his disdain for the holidays, nor was he worried about offending a potential business associate over differing views. But he couldn't quite bring himself to dim the sparkle in Hailey's eyes. Sharing his opinion of Christmas would be akin to telling a four-year-old that Santa was a sleighload of crap. Which was exactly what his stepmother-du-jour had done to him.

Instead, he did what he was best at. Sidestepped the question with a charming smile. "I promise you, I've never been called Grinchy in my life."

The speculation in her big eyes told him he might need to toss out a little more charming distraction. Otherwise, she seemed like the stubborn type. The kind who sweetly nagged at a person until they'd spilled their every secret, then thanked her for dragging them through the ugly memories.

"How about you?" he asked. "Why is an elf your favorite holiday character?"

"Elves are clever. They bring joy and create beauty, but they stay behind the scenes. They're the cute and cuddly part of the background." To emphasize her point, she offered a bright smile, tilted her chin toward her shoulder and twirled around so her skirt offered a tempting view of her stockings. Which, Gage's mouth watered to realize, were thigh-high and held up with garters.

"But elves don't have their own movie," he pointed out. "As grumpy as he is, even the Grinch gets top billing."

"*Elf* is a movie. And top billing usually comes with top headaches," she pointed out. "Expectations and demands of excellence. Appearances, groupies, haters. Is all of that really worth the spotlight?"

Gage frowned.

Hell, yeah, it was worth it. The other option sounded kind of…forgettable. Who aspired to that?

Maybe that was why she was an agent instead of striving to be the star, he guessed.

Still…

"Being on top is better than being on the bottom," he pointed out.

"Not always." Her words were low, teasing and lilting with innuendo. The look in her eyes was hot, sexy. And way more appreciative of the view than he figured his costume warranted. But who was he to dissuade a gorgeous woman from appreciating him?

His momma didn't raise no fools. Of course, she didn't raise her sons, either, but that was beside the point.

Right now, the point was seeing how hot this spark could flame between him and the deliciously naughty elf.

He stepped closer.

Amusement and desire both clear on her face, Hailey stepped back. With a quick glance over his shoulder, as if gauging their privacy, she wet her lips.

Gage almost groaned.

He probably could have walked away before.

Probably.

But now? Seeing that full mouth damp and inviting?

He wasn't leaving without a taste.

"Being on top has a few definite benefits," he decided quietly, now having completely switched places so her back was against the wall and his toward the ballroom.

"Does it? Like what?" Her eyes were huge, so big they were lost in the curls tumbling out from the white fur brim of her hat.

Need, stronger than any he'd felt over a simple flirtation, surged through Gage's body. He angled his body so Hailey was trapped between him and the wall.

For a second, one delicious second, he just stared.

Enjoyed the anticipation in her eyes.

The rapid pulse fluttering in her throat.

The tempting display of luscious flesh, mounded above the tight satin binding her breasts.

The need intensified. Took on a sharp, hungry edge.

"Like this," he said, giving in to its demand.

He took her mouth.

He'd intended to be gentle. Sweet, even.

But the kiss was carnal and raw and dancing on the edges of desperate. Tongues tangled. Lips slid, hot and wet.

She tasted as sweet as she looked.

But the sounds she made were sexual nirvana. Low, husky moans of approval as his hands skimmed over her waist to that tempting place just below her breasts. He didn't touch. He just tortured the both of them with the idea that he could.

Public, he forcibly reminded himself. They were practically in public, and if he did what he wanted, they'd be putting on a display for a ballroom full of people.

Knowing if he didn't stop now, that display was a very real possibility, Gage slowly, reluctantly, pulled his mouth from hers.

It was harder than he'd thought it'd be. And not just between his legs.

Unwilling to let go completely, his hands flat against the wall on either side of her head, Gage leaned closer. His body trapped hers as he pressed tiny kisses along her throat. Hailey's head fell back, her breath coming fast, filling the air with tiny bursts of white fog.

The move arched her back, so the long, delicious length of her throat was bare and those glorious breasts pressed higher against his chest. His hands burned with the need to cup her bounty. To weigh the soft flesh. To slide that candy-cane-striped fabric down and see if she was as tasty as he thought.

Public, Gage reminded himself again. *Keep it in control.*

Because while he wasn't averse to a little public display of passion himself, he had the feeling that Hailey would be. Especially if some of those models in there were hers.

Then her hands shifted, moving off his shoulders to press their way down his chest. Gage could feel their heat even through the thick fur of his costume.

He shuddered with need, taking in the flush of rosy color washing over Hailey's cheeks and pouring down her throat and chest to meet that tight satin.

One taste couldn't hurt, he decided.

Even as his mind listed all the ways it actually could, he moved closer, so his body was tight against hers. As Hailey's hum of pleasure filled the air, he pressed his mouth against the side of her throat, just under her ear, and gave in to the need to taste.

She was delicious.

Seriously worried for his sanity if she kept teasing him with those delicate fingers, Gage folded his hand over hers and pressed her palm flat against his chest. Then he grabbed the zipper tab and yanked.

It didn't move.

The grabby need clawing at Gage's libido slowed, even as the foggy desire tried to pull him back.

He yanked again.

Nothing.

"Hell," he muttered, pulling his mouth from Hailey's.

Unwilling to separate their bodies, he angled his head to peer at his chest. He got a better grip on the tab and pulled again.

The zipper was stuck.

"I can't get it down."

"Well, I guess I'd rather hear that than you can't get it up," she said, her eyes dancing with laughter. Clearly a smart woman, Hailey pressed those lush lips together to keep it contained, though.

Gage growled.

And yanked.

Nothing.

This was not happening.

His body straining against the thick fur of the costume from hell, he considered ripping it right off.

"I guess the moment's lost," he said with a reluctant smile when she couldn't hold back her laughter any longer. He figured that was better than acting like a spoiled, tantrum-throwing asshole.

Although he was reserving the right to throw the tantrum later in private.

"Maybe not lost," she said, her smile gentle now, her eyes bright with promise. "Maybe just delayed."

Gage considered the option of a delay over cancellation.

It had a lot more appeal. And while he wasn't so uptight that he had stupid rules about sex, clients and associates, he was also smart enough to know that women got funny about stuff. If Hailey thought he'd slept with her to get to her client, and to snag the deal, she'd go one of two ways. Give it to him because he was so damned good. Or with-hold it out of spite.

He didn't see her as the spiteful type, but she didn't come across as the kind of woman who'd take kindly to ulterior motives, either.

Time for some careful maneuvering.

"Why don't I call you?" he offered. After a quick men-tal review of his calendar, he added, "I'm out of town for the next couple of days. Are you available for dinner on Wednesday? I'll pick you up at six."

Her eyes were huge as she gave him a long look.

It was the kind of look that'd usually make him nervous.

A look filled with hope. With trust. With all those sweet, innocent emotions he'd never experienced in his life.

It was scary as hell.

His feet itched to run, even as his dick ached to stay.

"I have a meeting on Wednesday," she finally said. She reached up to trace her index finger over his lower lip, making Gage want to growl and nip at her soft flesh. Then, without warning, she ducked under his arm and shifted away.

Scowling at how lost his arms felt all of a sudden, he turned to watch her stop a couple of feet away. What? Did she think looking at her instead of touching was going to simmer down the need boiling through his system?

Impossible.

She was pure eye candy.

Still clinging with one hairpin, her hat was askew, dan-gling to one side. Blond curls, so soft when he'd tangled them in his fingers, were a bright halo around her face. And that face.

Gage wanted to groan.

He'd never gone for sweet. Sweet was dangerous. Sweet came with expectation, with demands. Sweet set off the run-don't-walk sirens in his head.

But he couldn't resist Hailey. He wanted all of the sweetness she had to offer.

But she was also the key to his winning this bet. And that, even more than the sirens, warned him to back off. At least until they'd settled their business.

"Well, if you have plans…" he started to say. Before he could excuse his way out of dinner and suggest a more businesslike meeting, she interrupted.

"Do you know Carinos?" she asked.

He gave a hesitant nod. Upscale and trendy, Carinos was the latest see-and-be-seen hot spot.

"How about I meet you there on Wednesday? We'll need to make it seven instead of six, though. I'm not sure how late my meeting will go."

This was it. His chance to back out.

But he couldn't make himself suggest alternate plans.

Gage tried to sort through his confused thoughts. Not an easy thing to do when he could barely stand, thanks to the throbbing hard-on he was sporting.

Before he could decide if he should accept or counter, she smiled.

That sweet, sexy smile that shut down his brain.

Looking like a naughty elf, Hailey wet her lips. He wanted to groan at the sight of her small, pink tongue.

And then, moving so fast she was a blur of blond, she kissed him. Hot, intense. A sweep of her tongue, a slide of her lips. Just enough hint of teeth to make him growl to keep from begging.

Then, before he could take control, or hell, even react

with more than a groan of appreciation for the hot spike of desire shooting through him, she moved back.

"See ya Wednesday," she said.

With that, a little finger wave and a smile that showed just a hint of nerves around the edges, she was gone.

Gage wanted to run after her. To grab her and insist she do something about the crazy desire she'd set to flames in his body.

Except for two things.

One, his dick was so hard, he couldn't walk for fear of something breaking.

And two, his mind was still reeling.

He'd tried to blame the costume. Because he didn't get stupid over women.

Ever.

But that cute little elf, with her candy-cane-sweet taste, had sent him so far into Stupidville, he might as well set up camp.

Until he'd figured it out, he needed to stay away from her.

Far, far away.

Because horny was all good and well.

And, he had to admit, stupid-horny was a pretty freaking awesome feeling.

But stupid-horny and business?

Not a good combination.

At least, not when his freedom was on the line.

4

"YOU'RE GRINNING LIKE a kid who just found a dancing pony under her Christmas tree. What's wrong with you?"

Wrong?

This was afterglow. Sexual anticipation. And a big ole dollop of nervous energy. It'd been three days since her kiss with Gage, and she was still floating.

Hailey inspected her image in the ornate standing mirror in the corner of her workroom-slash-office. Behind her were swaths of billowing silk, yards of lace and spilling bins of roses and romantic trim.

Only Doris would look at that and say it was wrong.

Hailey peered past her reflection to the woman behind her.

Doris Danson, or D.D. to her friends—which meant Hailey called her Doris—looked as if she were stuck in a time warp.

Rounded and a little droopy, her white hair was bundled in a messy bun reminiscent of a fifties showgirl. Bright blue eye shadow and false lashes added to the image. Doris's workday uniform consisted of polyester slacks, a T-shirt with a crude saying by a popular yellow bird and an appliqué holiday sweater complete with beribboned dogs, candy canes and sequin-covered trees.

The sweater and tee didn't bother Hailey. But as a designer, she was morally offended at the elastic-waisted polyester. Doris knew that. Hailey had a suspicion that the older woman haunted thrift stores and rummage sales to stock up on the ugly things.

"Nothing's wrong," Hailey said.

Not really. But she couldn't meet her secretary-slash-seamstress-slash-bookkeeper's gaze.

Despite her afterglow, she was kind of freaked out. She'd made out with a potential business associate. Now, granted, *associate* was a pretty loose term. But she was still walking a moral line here. Should Gage be off-limits? Maybe she shouldn't be obsessing over that kiss. Hailey bit her lip, chewing off the lip gloss she'd just slicked on five minutes ago.

"Might want to eat something besides your lipstick. Not like they feed you at these fancy meetings. Why you think it's a good idea to go talk to this guy after he burned you is a mystery, though."

"Mr. Rudolph didn't burn me. He'd never offered an actual contract. I'm sure I'll still get the exclusive. It's just going to be a little more interesting now." Jared and Trent wouldn't have praised her designs like they had if they didn't think she had the contract in the bag. And Hailey had a secret weapon now. A very sexy, very delicious one she was meeting for dinner.

"Interesting. Right. Instead of getting a solid deal you expected, you get to play some rich man's game." The wheels of her chair creaked as Doris shifted. The woman was barely visible behind the stacks of paper, catalogs and the tiny ceramic Christmas tree on her desk. Too bad she wasn't barely audible, too. "And where are you going to be when that other guy walks off with the contract? On the street, that's where."

Turning to give Doris a chiding look, Hailey insisted, "It's going to be fine. I'm going to get this deal."

Doris tut-tutted. "I'm telling you, Hailey, you are wasting your time. Better to accept reality than to keep dragging this out."

Hailey hated reality.

Especially when Doris dished it up with such bitter relish. It was as if she reveled in negativity. Hailey shifted her gaze from her own image to the woman behind her.

What a contrast.

Preparing for the meeting, Hailey was dressed in business chic. A black leather mini paired with leopard-print tights, a black silk turtleneck and a brushed cotton blazer with satin lapels. Along with her favorite boots and black knee-high schoolgirl socks, the look was savvy, sassy and modern. Just right for wowing a department-store tycoon and a fashion powerhouse.

And behind her was the elf of Christmas gloom.

An elf that knew the business inside and out, could finagle suppliers' fees down to pennies, worked magic with the books and, next to Hailey, was the best fill-in seamstress Merry Widow had ever seen. Which made her indispensable.

Indispensable gloom.

Not for the first time, she wished she were the kind of person who could tell Doris that her bad attitude wouldn't be tolerated and suggest the woman get her act together or clear out her desk.

But every time Hailey thought about doing it, she thought of everything the woman brought to the company. Then she remembered how lousy Doris's home life was, how Merry Widow was all she really had.

And whenever the older woman pissed her off so much that she forgot all that, the minute she got ready to get in her face, Hailey's tongue swelled up, her head buzzed with panic and she freaked out.

It wasn't that she was a wimp. She was a fierce negotiator in business, a savvy designer who insisted her company be run her way. She was smart. She was clever. She was strong.

She just sucked at confrontation.

Partially because her father had once told her that arguments always left scars. That even after making up, the memory of the conflict would forever change the relationship. Given that his advice had come on the heels of a hideous family drama that'd cost Hailey a whole year away from her new half brother, she'd taken the lesson to heart.

But mostly because she hated making people mad at her. Her mom had got mad and left her dad. Her dad got mad and refused to talk to Hailey. She'd seen plenty of mad in her life. Which was why she tried to avoid it like the plague.

"You want one of these cookies?" Doris asked, a frosted reindeer in hand. Doris shot Hailey a sour smile, bit the head off, then said around her mouthful, "Might as well eat up now, since things are gonna get tight after we go out of business."

"We're not going out of business," Hailey insisted, lifting a cream lace scarf to her shoulder to compare, then switching to one of vivid red cashmere.

"Right. Bet you still believe in Santa Claus, too."

"We're not going out of business," she said again. "Our sales are up ten percent over last year. Our projected first quarter should double that, easily."

"The Phillips kids are calling their daddy's note the first of the year," Doris reminded her like a persistently cheerful rain cloud.

Rotten kids. Or, really, greedy adults.

When Hailey had bought Merry Widow Lingerie from Eric Phillips three years ago, they'd agreed that he'd take a percentage of the profits for five years, with a final payment of the agreed-upon balance at the end of that time.

When he'd died in the fall, though, his kids had found a loophole in the contract, insisting that they could call the entire debt. They'd given Hailey until the end of the year, which was mighty big of them, in their opinion.

Without a significant contract the size of, oh, say Rudolph department stores, the bank wouldn't consider a loan in the sum the Phillipses were demanding.

Just thinking about it made Hailey's stomach churn, an inky panic coating the back of her throat.

No. She put the mental brakes to the freak-out. She wasn't going there. She'd found her answer; she just had to believe in it. She was going to snag this Rudolph-department-store contract.

Negative thinking, even the kind that had her second-guessing her date tonight, would only drag her down.

Giving her reflection a hard-eyed stare, Hailey vowed that she was going to rock this meeting and wow her date. As long as she didn't strip him naked and nibble on his body, she wasn't crossing any ethical work-relationship boundaries. Right?

Right.

Now she just had to get Doris off her back.

"When I pull in this department-store deal, we're golden. I can pay off the note, Merry Widow will be mine free and clear, and we'll be set," she assured the other woman.

"Do you bake special cookies to set out for Santa, or are you comfy settling for store bought? And those stars that fall from the sky, how many of those wishes actually come true for you?" Doris gave a pitying shake of her head. "You listen to me, miss. You keep going through life with your head in the clouds like you do, you're gonna fall in a big ole ditch one of these days."

What was it with the people in her life? Her mother was always warning that she'd get taken advantage of. Her friends worried that she was wearing rose-colored glasses. Even her father… Hailey bit her lip. Well, her father barely noticed what she was doing. But every once in a while, he did throw out a caution warning of his own. It wasn't as if she were Pollyanna with no clue. Hailey was a smart, perceptive woman. She'd made it to twenty-six without a major heartbreak, owned her own business and paid her bills on time. And unlike anyone else in her family, she hadn't had to resort to therapy and/or addictive substances along the way.

"I'm just saying, you might want to look at your alternatives. Me, I can retire anytime. But the rest of the team, don't they deserve a little heads-up so they can start looking for new jobs? It's all well and good to keep your hopes up," Doris said, her tone indicating the exact opposite. "But you can't let your Mary Sunshine attitude hurt other people, now, can you?"

"Everything is going to be fine. Why don't you focus on doing your job and let me do mine," Hailey snapped, her words so loud and insistent that the other woman dropped her cookie and stared.

She closed her eyes against Doris's shocked look. Hailey never snapped. In a life surrounded by simmering emotional volcanoes, she worked hard to be calm water. Mellow. Soothing, even. She'd grown up watching the devastation negativity and emotional turmoil caused, had spent her childhood trying to repair the damage.

And, of course, on the oh-so-rare occasions that she did respond to stress with a negative reaction, she always got that same horrified, might-as-well-have-kicked-a-puppy-and-cussed-out-a-nun look from people.

"I'm sorry," Hailey said with a grimace. "I'm just nervous about the meeting this afternoon. I want to make a good impression, to show Mr. Rudolph and his team that I'm the designer they want."

"You think the perfect scarf is going to make that dirty old man pick you as his lingerie designer?"

"I think the right look will show him my sense of style and savvy use of color and patterns," Hailey defended, lifting one scarf and then the other against her neckline again. "How a woman feels about her outfit affects her confidence, after all. If *I* think I look good, I'll project a strong image. And that might be all I need to get the deal."

"You might be a little overoptimistic about business stuff, but you've always had a firm handle on how well you put together fashion," Doris said with a frown. "Silly to start worrying about it now."

"I really want this contract." *Desperately needed it* was closer to the truth. But why put that fine a dot on the subject?

"An exclusive with the Rudolph department stores? It'll be so cool. The rich and famous shop there. They have a store on Rodeo Drive and everything. Can you imagine Gwyneth Paltrow in Sassy Class?" Hailey said in a dreamy tone, thinking of the pristine white satin chemise with delicate crocheted trim.

"Those highfalutin stars are the only ones who can afford to shop at snobby stores like Rudolph's." Doris's sniff made it perfectly clear what she thought of stars, snobs and all of their money.

"Well, unless you really do want to retire early and spend every day at home with your husband, you better cross your fingers that those snobs take to my designs," Hailey said, finally choosing the red scarf. It was sassier, she decided as she draped it elegantly around her neck. Frustrated, she wrinkled her nose. At least she was trying for elegant. It was hard when she'd knotted wrinkles into the scarf, so it looked like a soggy, deflated balloon around her neck.

Doris rolled her eyes, then hefted herself out from behind the desk to come over and adjust the scarf. A tug of fabric here, a tuck there, then she jerked her chin to indicate that Hailey turn back to the mirror.

While Doris fussed with the scarf, Hailey obsessed.

What if the other woman was right about it being impossible to come up with the funds to pay off the Phillips note?

What if Hailey's mother was right about Hailey shooting too high, wanting too much?

What if this was it, her last Christmas as the owner and head designer of Merry Widow Lingerie? What if it was the end of her dream?

"Not gonna happen," she muttered, lifting her chin to emphasize the promise.

"Whazzat?" Doris peered over her bifocals.

"Nothing," Hailey assured her in a cheery tone. With a smile to match, she patted the older woman's shoulder and promised, "Everything's great. Merry Widow is ready to fly, and this account is going to be our launchpad to make it happen."

The older woman harrumphed, but her usual grumpy look softened a little as she tucked one of Hailey's curls back into the faux chignon she'd fashioned at the base of her neck.

"Well, I will say this. If anyone deserves to make those dreams come true, you do." With that, and a stiff smile, Doris clomped back to her tin of cookies.

That was about the nicest thing Doris had ever said to her. It had to be a good omen, right?

Or the kiss of death.

An hour later, Hailey stepped into the glass elevator in the center of the Rudolph Building and pushed the button for the top floor. Top floor, baby. Unable to resist, she watched the surrounding buildings of the Financial District as the elevator rose, sighing when the sun broke through the clouds, and off in the distance she could just make out the Golden Gate Bridge. That had to be some kind of sign. Any day that included a meeting with a powerhouse like Rudolph, a pat on the back from Doris and a date with a sexy guy like Gage couldn't go wrong. Hailey practically skipped out of the elevator.

Still, she paused outside the frosted-glass double doors. One hand pressed to her stomach to calm her nerves, she took a deep breath. A quick glance at her feet to peek at her Jeffrey Campbells worked as a reminder that everything went better when a girl wore great boots. Then, resisting the urge to fluff her curls into frizz and nibble at her lipstick, she called up her brightest smile and pulled open the door.

This was it.

Her first foray into fashion fabulousness and the beginning of the best day of her life. A prelude, maybe, to the best *night* of her life.

With that peppy chant playing in her head, she swept into Rudolph Headquarters.

"Hailey, darling." Jared greeted her as soon as she crossed the foyer. He hurried around the high counter where he'd been chatting with the receptionist to offer a hug.

Hailey shifted, suddenly nervous.

"Hi, Jared. What's up?" He looked normal enough. Metro chic in his electric-blue suit and skinny tie, his hair slicked to the side and quirky horn rims perched on the bridge of his nose. But he was all tense, as if someone had just told him shoulder pads and moon boots were about to make a comeback.

"Up? Nothing, nothing. C'mon, let me escort you to the meeting. Rudy isn't in yet, of course. But you can get settled. I'll fetch you a nice latte, shall I?"

Hailey's stomach sank. Now she knew something was

wrong. Jared didn't fetch for anybody. She slowed, all but digging the spikes on the heels of her boots into the plush carpet to make Jared slow, too.

"Seriously. If something's happened…" She swallowed hard, then forced herself to continue. "If I've lost the account, I'd rather know before I go in that meeting."

Quick as a flash, a grimace came and went. Not a small feat considering the amount of Botox injected in that pretty face. "It's nothing, really. Just, well, Rudy finally got hold of Cherry Bella. She's interested, but not committed."

That sounded familiar. Hailey didn't figure reveling in the turned tables would endear her to Rudy, though. She kept her lips still.

"She's in tentative agreement, with the caveat that she gets to be the final judge on the various lines for the spring show. She and Rudy are nailing down those details."

"So how is this any different than it was Saturday night when he announced that it was a competition?" she wondered.

"Well, before we were pretty sure he was going to go with Merry Widow since he had this whole soft spring theme in mind. But Rudy apparently left the party Saturday with Vivo, the shoe designer."

So? Hailey arched both brows. She wasn't competing for the shoe contract.

"Vivo is edgy, modern and quirky. Think eight-inch platforms shaped like dinosaurs."

Eww, tacky. Halfway through her cringe, it hit her why Jared was so upset.

"Rudy's going to want the line to be a cohesive message…." Her words trailed off as it hit her.

Romantic sensuality didn't go with eight-inch platform dinosaurs. But snakeskin and black leather did.

And Rudy had a favor-wielding relationship with a designer who thought dinosaurs belonged on women's feet?

Anger ran, tense and jittery, along Hailey's spine. Fists clenched at her sides, she ground her teeth to keep from shouting that enough was enough. They kept changing the rules, shifting the playing field. Dammit, she deserved more respect than that. She'd worked hard for this deal, and until that stupid party, all indications were that she'd be awarded the contract.

She didn't say a word, though.

Yelling never helped anything. If she jumped all over Jared, it'd just make things uncomfortable, and might lose her whatever slim chance she had left.

Big picture, she reminded herself, taking deep breaths to try to push out the irritation. It was all about saving her company.

"I just found out a few minutes ago, or I'd have called to warn you. Cherry and Rudy are meeting with all of the designers together, listening to their pitches." Jared's words came at such a rush, they were spilling over themselves. Maybe because they'd reached the wide double doors of the meeting room.

"They're making the decision now?" she asked. Her fingers clutched her sassy messenger bag filled with marketing ideas and clever pitches aimed at the media. She'd come prepared to pitch the beauty of romantic lingerie that made women feel sexy. If she'd had more time, could she have found a way to work ugly shoes into her presentation? To show that even with the hideous footwear, a woman could still feel attractive?

His hand on the door, Jared closed his eyes for a second, as if he was fighting some inner battle. Then he leaned close and gave Hailey an intense look.

"Focus on Cherry. She's the key. Rudy will ignore his preferences in favor of whatever she likes, so chat her up. Make friends. She's on edge about something. Don't know if that's her typical personality or if she's having issues.

But she seems to be responding better to soft sells than hard pushes."

Before Hailey could process all of that, before she could do more than give Jared a grateful smile since she knew he was risking his job by showing preferential treatment, he'd pushed the door open and gestured her inside.

She wanted to grab his hand and drag him in with her.

But she didn't.

Instead, she took a deep breath of her own, lifted her chin, pulled back her shoulders and plastered on her best soft-sell smile.

Then, with as much enthusiasm as if there were a bed of hissing vipers on the other side, she swept over the threshold.

And almost tripped over her gorgeous boots.

"Hi," she breathed, the word taking all the air from her lungs.

GAGE SHIFTED HIS glare from the window to the door, ready to get this damned meeting over with.

And, for one of the few times in his life, found himself speechless. He had to blink a couple of times to make sure he wasn't seeing things, then found his voice.

"Hailey?"

Damn, she was pretty.

Her hair, still a froth of blond curls, was tamer than it'd been at the party. Sleeker, as if she'd bribed the curls into behaving by tying them in a knot at the base of her neck. Her big, round eyes were subtly made up, her lips pale and glistening. She was definitely looking more nice than naughty today.

But even without a candy-cane-striped bustier and thigh-grazing ballerina skirt, her sweet curves were mouthwatering. Instead of skimpy holiday wear, today she was decked out in a simple black skirt a few inches short of her knees and another pair of sexy boots. Her scarf and turtleneck screamed class, while her leopard-print tights assured him she was all sass.

He'd never been a foot-fetish kind of guy, but he was starting to seriously wonder what other styles of footwear she had in her closet. And how she'd look riding his body wearing just a pair of boots in thigh-hugging black leather.

"Gage?" Frowning, she chewed on the full pillow of her bottom lip, making him want to offer to take over the task. Then, as if she'd realized something, her eyes cleared and she offered a smile. "I didn't expect to see you."

"I'm surprised you recognized me without the green fur," he said with a teasing smile, walking across the room. He met her wide-eyed look with a wink.

He swept his gaze down her body again, noting the edgy boots and knee socks paired with tights and black leather.

She was a study in contrasts.

"Your suit is a definite step up from that costume," she agreed. "I'm glad to see you finally got the zipper unstuck."

She gave him a once-over just as hot as the one he'd given her. Her gaze slowed when passing over his faulty-zipper zone, making him wonder if he'd be having issues with these slacks. The speed at which she inspired an erection was hell on his clothes.

"I didn't. I had to cut the costume off."

"Oh." Her eyes danced with amusement, but she pressed her lips together in an attempt to keep from laughing aloud.

She was so damned cute.

He wanted to lift her off her feet and pull that curvy body against his, to see if it fit as good as he'd spent the weekend imagining. Not for the first time, he cursed his brother, the bet and that damned Grinch costume. If it weren't for Saturday night's thick layer of green fur— and a faulty zipper—he'd already know what she felt like.

But this was a formal meeting.

In someone else's office.

Getting hot and heavy with a business associate was definitely on the stupid list. Especially since Rudolph was likely to walk in at any moment. If he caught Gage and Hailey making out, he'd probably grab a video recorder and put it up on the company's YouTube channel.

So reluctantly, Gage offered his hand instead. The delicate softness of her palm and her quick intake of breath reminded him that she was about as close to an innocent as he'd been since his teens.

Maybe this was a bad idea.

"I didn't realize you were going to be a part of the meeting," she said breathlessly, her hand still nestled in his.

Gage frowned.

Why wouldn't he be here? This meeting was supposed to be him, Rudy, that singer chick and the competing designer. He'd figured he'd play to Rudy's good-old-boy persona while pitching circles around the designer. Milano's leather designs already appealed to Rudy's misogynistic perverted side. All Gage had to do was play that up, maybe intimidate the other designer a little and snag the contract on his way out the door to meet Hailey for dinner.

A dinner he'd been of two minds about keeping.

Hailey was everything he liked in a woman.

Sexy, fun and sporting a body that'd starred in all his dreams since the party.

And Hailey was everything he avoided in a woman.

Sweet, trusting and sporting an emotional innocence that promised nothing but trouble down the road.

And she was a business associate. Distant, perhaps, but still close enough to this project for it to possibly get messy. If he were smart, he'd offer a clever excuse and get out of their date. He'd keep this business deal simple, and himself out of trouble.

Gage was damned smart.

And here he had a chance to pitch to the singer's agent, just him alone. Might as well use it. Maybe it'd help keep his mind off stripping Hailey bare of everything but those boots.

"Since Rudolph is late, why don't we get comfortable? You can fill me in on what you think Cherry Bella likes best. And, of course, tell me what you're wearing under that skirt."

So much for keeping his mind off her naked.

Eyes wide, Hailey's mouth rounded to a surprised O before she let out a gurgle of laughter. As he escorted her to one of the half dozen club chairs by the window, she slanted him a teasing look.

"Under this? What better under leather than lace? Merry Widow lace, of course."

Releasing her elbow, Gage frowned.

What the hell?

She wore the competition?

"I'm a little confused," she said before he could point out the blatant conflict of interest. "Wouldn't you know better than I what Cherry likes?"

Why would he?

Gage gave Hailey a hard look.

Before he could ask exactly what her connection to Cherry, and to Rudolph, was, the department-store mogul swanned in with all but bugles blaring a fanfare. The small, bald man apparently made up for his lack of stature by surrounding himself with as big an entourage as possible. Mostly made up of busty women in short skirts, Gage noted. Two carrying briefcases, one with coffee and another with a tray of tiny pastries.

The women paraded in, each setting her item on a wide, glass-topped table, then without a word, doing a snappy about-face and parading right back out.

Leaving Hailey to stare, wide-eyed, Gage frowning and Rudolph posing in the doorway. And Cherry Bella nowhere to be found.

Was that why Hailey was here? To rep her client?

"Darlings, I'm late. So let's not dawdle. Sit, sit." Rudolph waved his fingers at Gage, who, after a second's debate, sat. But opposite Hailey instead of next to her. He had a feeling he was going to get more out of watching her face than whatever the old coot spouted.

"It'll just be the three of us, I'm afraid." As if to emphasize his statement, he came over to sit with them, rat-a-tat-tatting his fingers on his knee and frowning. "I know you're both anxious to hear the decision of who'll be awarded the contract. I'd intended to give it today, with Cherry's help. But as she's ill, we'll have to reconvene tomorrow."

"Tomorrow?" Tension spiked Gage's system. And not the happy, sexual kind he'd been enjoying thanks to Hailey. This meeting was supposed to finish up his commitments to Milano for the year. He had his own clients to see, several projects in the works. He didn't have time to play babysitter to a leather lingerie line and a kooky, old guy.

"Unfortunately, Cherry felt ill after lunch," the old guy said, sounding more irritated than sorry. "She apologizes for missing the meeting, but insists on talking with the designers herself and having a say in the decision if she's to take the role of spokesmodel. I hate to inconvenience you, but we'll have to meet again tomorrow. Cherry feels the lingerie is the linchpin of her agreement to signing on as the face of Rudolph for next year."

Gage barely heard a thing after the words *talking with the designers.* His eyes shifted to Hailey. Her eyes were round, those full lips parted in a silent gasp. Not a gasp of pleasure, either.

Nope. She looked about as horrified as he felt.

"Inconvenient for the two of you, but as much as I'm sure you both want this contract, I'm sure you'll make adjustments." With that pronouncement of misperception, Rudy bounced up and scurried over to the tray-topped table. "So are you in the mood for cocoa? And a sweet, of course. What's Christmas without cookies? Then we'll take a quick look at the test shots my photographer took of Cherry in each of your designs. Consider it an early gift, since it gives you a chance to refine the pitch you'll need tomorrow."

Hailey closed her eyes, taking a deep breath, then shaking her head as if trying to shift the new facts into the old picture. If the pinched expression on her face was any indication, she wasn't liking the way it looked now.

Gage could relate.

Son of a bitch.

There went his Christmas treat.

5

WELL, THIS DAY had totally sucked.

Sinking deeper into the worn booth, Hailey looked around the retro diner and took a deep breath to keep from crying. Then wrinkled her nose as the acrid scent of burning burger filled the air. On opposite sides of the room, two babies screamed their dissatisfaction with dinner, their cries echoing off the curved glass window in stereo.

Carinos this wasn't.

Of course, there was nothing to celebrate, either. So a cheap diner was much more fitting than a four-star restaurant.

She wanted that account. She'd worked her ass off for it. She was damned good, her designs were high quality and on trend, yet unique and memorable. Her costs were reasonable, her profit margin solid. She'd put together a fabulous proposal.

She was perfect for Rudolph's spring line.

Her designs were perfect for Cherry Bella.

Now she was afraid perfect might not be enough. That this time, just like so many others, she'd get within touching distance to getting what she wanted, only to have it swept away.

She glared at the glass on the table in front of her.

Other than being made of melted sand, it in no way resembled the sexy, seductive wineglass she'd thought she'd be sipping from right now while flirting her way through a very promising date.

Nope, this glass was thick, with hot fudge sliding down one side and a puddle of melting, sprinkle-embedded whipped cream pooling on the stem.

She licked a smudge of chocolate off her knuckle, taking comfort from the bittersweet richness.

She was wearing her favorite lingerie under this chic outfit. A sweet, dove-gray demi bra with picot lace and tiny pink satin rosebuds. She'd imagined describing the matching thong and garter belt to Gage over candlelight and appetizers, letting that image set the tone for the rest of their evening.

Her garter belt pressed tight against her overfull tummy, a reminder of just how mistaken she'd been. No pleasant alcohol buzz and sexual zing happening here for her.

Instead, she had an ice-cream gut ache and felt as if she'd been beaten around by a bag full of gloom. Heck, she could give Doris a run for her money for the biggest downer award in this mood.

And it was all Gage Milano's fault.

As if her thoughts, or an ice-cream-inspired fantasy, had called him up, Gage suddenly appeared right there at her booth.

Sexy as hell, his black hair windswept from the chilly San Francisco weather and tumbling over his forehead in a way that made her fingers itch to tidy it. His eyes were intense, wicked and amused as he arched one brow. And his body. Yes, he was wearing a leather bomber jacket, so she didn't have full view of those delicious shoulders. But hey, she'd correctly pegged how gorgeous they were when he was draped in green fur. She could imagine them just fine covered in leather.

Leather.

Something he specialized in.

Hailey blinked a few times, sure he was just a sugar mirage. But he didn't disappear. Instead, he smiled.

Damn him. And he didn't even have the courtesy to look out of place. Instead, he was perfectly at ease. It was so irritating.

"What are you doing here?" she asked.

"I followed you."

She shook her head. No, he hadn't. She'd been here, stuffing her face and getting sick on ice cream, for almost three-quarters of an hour. Her body would have sent up horny signals if he was anywhere near her.

"I'd have been in sooner, but once I saw you were settling here for a bit, I had to make some phone calls."

Perfectly at ease and acting as if he had no doubt she'd be thrilled to see him, Gage shrugged out of his jacket and slipped into the seat opposite her. She was distracted from feasting her eyes on his shoulders when, with a grimace, he shifted to lift one hip, then slid back toward the seat's edge. Hailey smirked at the contrast of his sleek looks cozied up in an ice cream and burger booth. She hoped his hundred-dollar slacks had just got stuck in a chocolate smear.

Was that mean of her?

Sure.

But dammit, she'd really been looking forward to their date—and the sex she'd imagined they'd be having soon afterward.

Talk about disappointed.

It was like every Christmas she could remember.

She'd be promised something wonderful, be it that special gift from Santa or her parents not fighting for one blessed day. She'd spend the entire season winding herself up with excitement, hoping and imagining just how amazing it would be.

And, always, it'd been a huge disappointment.

Santa never brought her what she asked for.

Her family never kept their promises.

And her prettily imagined holiday never came true.

She knew it wasn't really Gage's fault. He hadn't known they were in competition for the contract, either. But she couldn't help but feel that the Grinch had, indeed, stolen her Christmas.

"Why'd you follow me?" For one tiny second she imagined maybe it was to beg her to go out with him still. To tell her how hot he was for her, that a silly thing like business shouldn't stand between what they'd felt for each other.

"I thought we should talk. Maybe work this out between us." His smile was pure charm, his look so potent that—despite her vow that he was now off-limits—she was tempted to start undressing right then and there.

"Really?" Her pulse joined the dance and Hailey shifted in her seat, her waistband a little snug from holding her breath—and all that ice cream.

"Really." He leaned forward and lifted her hand into his. His thumb rubbed along the center of her palm, heating and stirring. "I figure there's no reason we can't both have what we want, right?"

Her mouth was too dry for words, so she settled on a nod. He was so damned sexy. His eyes were hypnotic, as if he was trying to pull her in. She didn't think it'd take much for her to follow just about any suggestion he might offer up.

"I mean, who knows what kind of crazy things Rudolph might want in order to award the contract. Look at how he's dragged this out already. First he was supposed to announce the lineup on Saturday. Then it was today. Now it may be tomorrow. I know you're a busy lady, and I definitely have plenty on my schedule. So why don't we make this easy for him. What do you say?"

"What?"

Her pulse slowed to a thud, matching the feeling of anticipation deflating in her belly.

"How about I make you an offer? Hook you up with some other potential clients, some big names. A half dozen hot leads you could nail down before the weekend. And, probably, before Rudolph would get around to figuring out what he wants." Gage added a charming smile, as if he were plopping a fat, juicy cherry on top of his delicious proposition.

Delicious, that was, for him. She clenched her teeth against the rude words she wanted to spew, leaving a sick taste in her mouth.

When she didn't answer, he craned his head forward to check out her ice cream, then lifted a spoon from the place setting on his side and scooped up a bite.

"Not a bad chocolate," he commented. "I'd have pegged you as a more adventurous ice-cream connoisseur, though. Espresso, some exotic fruit or maybe bourbon flavored."

"But then, you don't know me very well, do you?"

Brows arched, he gave a slow nod and set the spoon down. He had a look of smug satisfaction on his face. As if he'd just been proved right about something.

"I know more about you than I did before," he offered, his smile so full of charm it was dripping in her ice cream. "You're an up-and-coming force to be reckoned with. Your designs are pure romance, created to make any woman and every woman feel sexy."

"How sweet." She reached forward with two fingers and slid her glass of leftover melted ice cream back toward her, out of his reach. "You memorized my promotional materials. Did you also notice that my designs are the perfect look for Cherry Bella?"

"Well, c'mon," he said, his smile teasing and light, even though his eyes were narrowed now, a little more watchful and a little less charming. "Cherry Bella's the kind of woman who can wear anything and make it look great. And she's going to be the total focus of the spring line. The clothes will barely be noticed."

"My designs always get noticed."

"Sure they do. I'm not saying they're not great. They are. But c'mon, we both know leather gets more looks than froth."

He was so sure he was going to win, he'd just given her the pity look. The oh-so-sorry-you're-a-distant-second look. She'd seen that look so often in her life, she'd have thought she was immune.

Except when it was on Gage's face.

Her jaw tight, Hailey had to work to keep her expression polite, when all she wanted to do was stick out her tongue, dump her melted ice cream in his lap and storm out.

She'd be damned if the sexiest man she'd ever met was going to think she wasn't good enough. Even if he was no longer in the running to find out just how good she *really* was.

"Are you trying to say my designs aren't good enough to get this deal when they're up against yours?"

"I didn't say that." His frown was a flash, gone in a blink. But she caught the surprise in it and realized he'd not only thought she wasn't good enough, he'd also thought she was a wimp-girl. As fluffy and frothy and fragile as her designs.

A lifetime of never being quite enough had, if nothing else, taught her to fight like hell for what she wanted. So before he could respond, she leaned forward and offered her sexiest smile. Her eyes locked on his, she trailed her fingers over the back of his hand in a soft, teasing gesture, then arched her brow.

"But that's what you meant." Hiding both her hurt and her frustration, she gave a pitying shake of her head. "A shame, really. Because if you'd played your cards differ-

ently, you'd have been able to find out firsthand just how
fabulous my lingerie is."

VISIONS OF HAILEY'S curvy little body packaged in shim-
mering lace and delicate ribbons danced through Gage's
brain like tempting sugarplums.

Visions he'd been damned close to seeing in real life.

He'd been so sure when he walked in here that he could
charm her into stepping aside. He'd made a few phone
calls, called in a couple of favors and lined up a handful
of potential clients for her. Nothing as big as Rudolph in
terms of prestige. But some solid deals that could keep her
in sexy shoes for a while.

She had a good product, but she was still up-and-
coming. Not quite in the same league as Milano. He'd
figured she'd be so grateful, they'd not only keep their
dinner date, but hurry right through so they could get to
the dessert he'd been thinking about.

All he had to do was dish up a little charm, weave his
marketing magic and ta-da. He'd be licking chocolate off
her belly.

Instead, he'd barely warmed up when Hailey flashed
those big green eyes at him and he'd totally forgotten his
plan. That had never happened before. He'd had women
flash their breasts in the middle of a sales pitch and he
hadn't missed a beat.

But now, with his freedom on the line, he'd stepped all
over his own tongue. Nothing like coming off as an arro-
gant ass to tip his hand and piss her off. He'd already lost
his shot at seeing her naked. Time to table the idea of dinner, and dessert, and just get her to agree to give up the
Rudolph deal. That way he could get the contracts nailed
down before ole Rudy decided to add another twist or drag
it out further. Then Gage could keep his own client ap-
pointments and maybe still get in a little holiday vacation.

Noting the chill in her eyes as she pulled out her wallet to pay for the ice cream, he figured he'd better do it before she walked out.

It was going to take some quick talking.

And some clever marketing.

Good thing he was good at both.

"I already know firsthand how great your lingerie is." He waited a beat, enjoying the way her eyes widened and a hint of pink touched her cheeks. Unable to resist, his gaze dropped to her chest. Completely covered to her chin in a black turtleneck, he could still imagine how she'd looked Saturday night. "You have a distinct sense of style, and now that I think about it, your elf outfit featured pieces of your lingerie line, didn't it?"

Like that bustier. The candy-cane-striped one that'd made his tongue ache to lick her.

"It did," she agreed slowly, as if not sure she wanted to trust him. Gage had to hand it to her; she looked like a china doll, but she was damned smart.

"I'm impressed. Most men don't notice what a girl's wearing, let alone remember and recognize pieces of it days later."

"You made quite an impression. Even if I'd known we were competitors, I'm sure I'd still have hit on you, but I might have been a little more aware that this could get awkward."

"Oh, I don't know," she said, her words as sweet as the hot fudge on the edge of the ice-cream glass. She reached out to touch her finger to the thick chocolate, then pressed it to her tongue. His brain shut down. Gage didn't know whether she'd done it because she was nervous or because she just knew it was the perfect way to torture him. Either way, the south side of his body took a quick leap north.

"You don't know?" he repeated, totally forgetting what they'd been discussing. Something about lingerie, probably.

"I don't know that this is awkward, really. More like a disappointment. I mean, we're both trying to win the same contract. That means our dinner date is off." As Gage was trying to find some appreciation for her practical acceptance of that, she gave a deep sigh that pressed her full chest against that lucky black fabric—and made the blood flow to his dick.

It was that rush of blood that inspired his next words.

"I don't think it has to be quite as cut-and-dried as that," he argued. "You can take my offer, reel in some big clients and everyone's happy. Then we can play the rest of the game just fine."

"You see this as a game?"

"The contract?" he asked. "Or our date?"

Her laugh was a soft puff of air, barely there and not enough to reach her eyes.

"Well, I guess that answers that."

"I'm just saying I don't think we need to let this contract business get in the way of any potential pleasure between us," he heard himself propositioning. This was the first time his dick had ever taken direct control of his brain and had him saying things he knew were insane. Gage wasn't sure if he should be impressed or terrified.

"Well, that does sound tempting," Hailey agreed, her look so warm and sexy that he decided terrified was the wisest choice.

"But I've got to ask," she continued, turning the ice-cream glass in slow circles, its tempting fudge and just a smidgen of whipped cream on the side making him crazy with hunger. "Are you comfortable in second place? Because I plan to win that contract."

It took him three whole seconds to rip his gaze off her full lips and realize what she'd said.

She thought she could beat him?

Hell, all she had to do was take a deep breath and he'd be so focused on her body, she just might have a shot at it.

"Babe, you might want to rethink your plan." Despite feeling as if he'd fallen off a very unfamiliar cliff, Gage gave her a cocky smile. "I never lose."

He knew that statement edged him over into total ass territory. But dammit, he was rattled.

Since this was a first, he clearly wasn't handling it well.

"Rethink my plan?" Her thick lashes fluttered over those big, round eyes, but she didn't look intimidated. Nope. If anything, Hailey appeared irritated. "In what way do you think it needs rethunk?"

Was that even a word? From the way she'd lifted her sharp chin, and arched one brow, Hailey looked as though she was challenging him to question it.

Gage shook his head, trying to bring his thoughts back in line. This wasn't about words, silly or otherwise. This was about her potential disappointment.

He might have had to kiss goodbye all of the prurient sexual plans he had for her body, but he wasn't the kind of guy who took his disappointment out on a lady.

He liked to think he was too chivalrous for that.

So he decided to warn her instead. Hopefully keep her from getting her hopes up too high.

"You're clearly the kind of gal who throws herself into things wholeheartedly," he observed. From the tiny furrow between her brows, he figured he'd hit the mark, and she wasn't exactly thrilled to be read that easily. No surprise. Most of his competitors weren't. "But in this case, you'd do better to have a backup plan."

"Because you're so sure you're going to win."

"I'm just saying I don't want to see you disappointed," he told her, his smile as soothing as the hand he gently glided over her arm.

Her green eyes chilled and she shifted her arm to one

side. Only a few inches, but enough to make it clear that touching her had just made the off-limits list.

"Ooh," she said, drawing the word out in a husky tone that made him think of bedtime moans and whispered words in the dark. She tilted her head to one side and nodded. "So you don't want me to be disappointed."

Never taking her eyes from his, she grabbed her jacket and purse from the seat beside her and slid from the booth. Her body moved with a grace that made it impossible for him to look away, even as manners automatically kicked in and sent him to his feet, as well.

Her lips flicked in a satisfied smile, as if she'd expected nothing less.

Then, in a move as deliberate as it was bold, her gaze slowly—oh, baby, so painfully slowly—drifted down his body. When she reached his zipper, and every wonderful thing contained therein, she gave a sad sort of shake of her head, then looked him in the eye.

"Since our date, and any other plans that it might have led to, are clearly canceled, I'm sure the odds of my being disappointed just plummeted."

With that perfect put-down, and a smile more wicked than a woman with a face as sweet as hers should be allowed, Hailey turned on one sexy heel and walked away.

Leaving Gage to stare at her very fine ass while trying to pull his jaw off the floor.

6

THE MAN WAS pond scum. Worse, he was sexy pond scum disguised as temptation. And he was so damned sure he was going to sweep in and snag the contract. Hailey ground her teeth, still pissed. A good night's sleep might have helped, but she'd spent the night having erotic dreams of Gage, covered in sexy pond scum that looked a lot like his Grinch fur.

Damn him.

There was no way she was letting him take this contract from her. No way in hell.

Hailey stepped into Rudy Rudolph's office riding high on a righteous anger, a double caramel latte and the feminine confidence only great lingerie and a new pair of shoes could offer.

The black leather of her double-strap Mary Janes was a perfect contrast to her red tights and purple knit slip dress. She'd offset the aggressive colors by pulling her hair back in a loose braid, letting tendrils curl around her face. As accents, she'd assured herself. Not for something to hide behind.

"Miss North, welcome."

"Call me Hailey," she told the bald little man for the tenth time. Her smile stiffened when she saw that Gage was already there.

Not only there, she noted, narrowing her eyes. But there, cozied up in the seating area by the window. Right next to a buxom redhead who looked as if she ate sexy guys for breakfast and snacked on the more adventurous ones for dessert.

Hailey's fashion eye took in the woman's expensive dress, a Zac Posen cloque in gunmetal, paired with a droolworthy pair of matching Louboutins. You couldn't begrudge the woman's excellent taste. In clothes, shoes or—Hailey noted as the redhead reached over to lay her hand on Gage's wrist—in men.

"Have a seat, Hailey. Can I get you a drink?"

Gage and the redhead still ignoring her, Hailey refused Rudy's offer, her fingers gripping her leather portfolio bag's handle so tight she was surprised the stitches didn't fall out.

"Cherry," Rudy called as he ushered Hailey across the room. "Here she is. The owner and designer of Merry Widow Lingerie, Hailey North. As you can see, she's just as fetching as her designs."

The redhead rose, a slow sinuous move that in the end had her towering over Hailey's petite frame. It was easy to see why Rudolph wanted her as the face of his spring campaign. She was the embodiment of smoldering sexuality.

"It's a pleasure to meet you, Miss Bella," Hailey said, her words stiffer than she'd like. Because Gage was giving her that smug look, she told herself. Not because the woman had just been touching a guy Hailey herself wanted to lick like a melting Popsicle.

"I love your designs," Cherry said, her trademark voice husky and low, more suited for a dim, smoky bar than a business meeting. But her smile was genuine, and her grasp warm and friendly as she took Hailey's hand. Not to shake. Just to hold for a second, as if making a connection while pulling her over and gesturing that Hailey take the seat next to her. "You create the most romantic celebration of femininity I've ever seen. I'm awed."

Oh.

Her throat tightened. It was enough to make a girl cry.

"And such a contrast to the raw power of Milano's designs," Cherry continued, sliding into her chair with a boneless sort of grace. "Also a celebration of the female form, but with a very different message."

And that was enough to make a girl want to throw things.

For once, just once, Hailey wanted to be the clear choice. The one someone wanted most. But hey, a lifetime of coming in second, third and fourth best taught a girl a few things about sticking with it.

So she kept her big smile in place and sat, not nearly as gracefully, beside Cherry.

"If you don't mind my asking, which do you think suits you best?" Hailey heard herself ask. She barely refrained from biting her lip to try to snap the words back. She'd planned to be charming, persuasive and subtle. Like her designs.

But Cherry didn't seem offended. Instead, she laughed and gave a noncommittal shrug. "I'm a multifaceted woman. Choosing isn't a simple thing. Much, always, depends on my mood."

Hailey almost pointed out that her designs suited a variety of moods, while Milano's only suited the kinkier ones. But this time she managed to keep her mouth closed.

Instead, she—finally—let herself look at Gage.

His dark eyes were aimed right at her, a small smile playing over those sexy lips. As if he were looking into her mind and poking through her plans and ideas, preparing to blow them all to teeny-tiny pieces.

Yet, she still wanted him.

If she closed her eyes, she could still taste that kiss.

Could still feel the touch of his fingers against her skin. Remember the scent of his cologne, the feel of his hair.

No, no, no. The man was a shark, she reminded herself. Not Prince Charming. He'd eat her up in one bite.

An idea which really shouldn't turn her on.

"Let's get started, shall we? Cherry's expressed her preferences between the other choices." Rudy went on to name the lines Cherry had chosen.

Hailey almost jumped out of her chair to do a happy dance when Vivo wasn't among them. They were all strong designers, but none so out there that her lingerie wouldn't complement them. Of course, none were so conservative that Milano's wouldn't work, either. But Hailey was going to ignore that for right now.

"Yours is the final line Cherry needs to review before we settle on the spring lineup," Rudy continued. Playing waiter with a dapper flair, he set a Plexiglas tray on the small table centered between their four chairs, motioned to the coffee, tea and juice as if encouraging everyone to help themselves.

When nobody did, he snagged a Christmas cookie shaped like a reindeer, bit its head off and gestured with its body. "I'd like the two of you to give a final pitch. Tell us why your design is perfect for Cherry Bella and Rudolph department stores."

"Ladies first," Gage said before Hailey could do more than take a nervous breath.

She gave him a look, intending to say something— anything—that'd put him in his place and let him know that he wasn't running this show.

But the second her eyes met his, her brain shut down. She hated that. But her body—oh, her body—it loved the results. Big-time.

Her heart did a little dance in perfect time with the nerves swirling around in her stomach. She could stare into his eyes for hours. Days, even. Nights would be even better. She wanted to see those eyes heat again, darken with desire and smolder with passion. Like they'd done when he'd kissed her.

She wet her lips, remembering his taste. The texture of his mouth. The sweep of his tongue.

"Hailey?"

"Hmm?" She blinked. Then she blinked again, her eyes widening in horror before she ripped them from Gage to focus on the man with the giant checkbook and the key to her future. "I'm sorry, what?"

"Why don't you go ahead and make your pitch."

She wanted to suggest that Gage go first instead. She wanted to ask for a bucket of ice. She could barely think straight with her brain locked in horny mode. But they were all gazing at her expectantly and she didn't want to make waves. Or worse, look as though she wasn't grateful for this opportunity.

Deep breaths and don't look at Gage, she instructed herself.

Okay, then…

She'd spent all night obsessing over this. Now that it was time to pitch it, she hoped like hell she'd obsessed in the right direction.

"Clearly you have two very strong lingerie lines to choose from," Hailey said, starting her pitch by offering Gage her first smile, then going right back to trying to pretend he wasn't there. "The question is, which one do you think is going to garner the best publicity and success for both Rudolph department stores and for Cherry Bella?

"Your theme for spring is A New You. Your strategy is to inspire makeovers, redos and taking chances. And where better to begin such a journey than with how a woman feels about herself. Lingerie goes beyond physical support. It provides emotional support. The right lingerie inspires a woman to believe in herself. It validates her femininity. Merry Widow Lingerie is more than a fashion statement. It's an empowerment statement."

Hailey paused, gauging their expressions. The interest in Rudy's combined with the agreement in Cherry's was great. But it was the concern on Gage's that rocked her. With that as encouragement, she continued her presentation. She pulled out graphs and sales figures, passed around a few samples of the merchandise in all its frothy lace beauty and put her entire heart into the pitch.

"It really comes down to messaging," she wound up. "What message do you want to send women, and what message do you think women will respond best to? I think you'll find that romance, with its empowering belief in love and happy results, will be a stronger selling point."

Pleased with her speech, and that she could sit back down and pretend she wasn't nervous enough to hurl, Hailey offered Rudy and Cherry a warm smile. Then, her body boneless, she slid into the chair next to Gage's. As soon as she did, he stood. Clearly he wanted to erase her impression as quickly as possible from the others' minds.

"Since it's just the four of us, let's be honest," Gage said in a persuasively amused tone. "We all know what sells. Especially when it comes to lingerie."

"And that is?" Cherry asked, clearly not willing to let him take the easy way through his pitch.

"Sex. Empowerment and emotions are all great between the pages of a book or at a self-help seminar. But nobody thinks that when they are buying lingerie. What women, and more importantly men, are thinking about when they look for lingerie is sex."

Hailey's mouth dropped open. It took her a solid five seconds to force it closed.

He'd thrown her under the bus. For the first time since she'd seen him all wrapped up in that green fur costume, she wanted to kick him. Gage wasn't the Grinch, she realized. He was a flat-out shark. A shark standing there in a very expensive suit, looking as though he owned the whole damned world.

"Now, as sweet and appealing as Merry Widow's lingerie is, let's face it…there's nothing that says sex like black leather." To emphasize his point, Gage lifted a presentation board from his portfolio and continued his pitch. Hailey barely heard him, though; she was too busy focusing on the photo of a leggy redheaded model swathed in leather and holding a microphone, a blatant play to Cherry.

To try to keep from hissing at being dismissed as sweet and appealing, as if those were stupid things, Hailey shifted her gaze toward Rudy and Cherry. Were they as disgusted by the hard sell as she was?

Her stomach sank.

Instead of disagreeing, Rudy was nodding away, his eyes on the leather-clad model's photos and his tongue practically draped over his tie.

And Cherry… Well, she was staring out the window, her expression as far away and morose as the gray clouds engulfing the bridge.

Gage just kept on pitching, reiterating and reframing the presentation he'd offered ten minutes before. He alternated between numbers that seemed to make Rudy drool and flattery that, thankfully, Cherry wasn't paying much attention to. Instead, the woman looked pensive as she stared out the window.

Her teeth clenched, Hailey wanted to yell *no.* They were smart business people, weren't they? Shouldn't this decision be based on an overall logic? On what fit best for the line? On the designs that'd appeal to the widest demographic?

As Gage finished his pitch, sliding the cover over his presentation board and taking a seat, Rudy's decision was clear on his face. Hailey's heart sank into her very cute shoes. He was clearly a man who'd made his fortune thinking a little south of logic.

"Well, thank you both. This was a very informative morning," the older man said. "Why don't we break for lunch now so Cherry and I can discuss this, and we'll notify you by this afternoon of our decision."

Her stomach plunged into her adorable shoes fast enough to make Hailey nauseous.

He was going to choose Milano. Despite the fact that Cherry had overruled his preference, Vivo's shoe designs, he was still going to pick the ugly leather.

And that would mean the end of Merry Widow Lingerie.

Oh, sure, she could eventually get a job doing design elsewhere. Maybe. But what about her employees? Her clients? Her dream?

She took a deep breath, trying to accept that she couldn't change the man's mind. She couldn't jump up, stomp her feet and insist he choose her. She'd tried that a few times over the course of her life, and had always been the one standing there alone with sore toes.

But…

She couldn't just let it go.

"Wait," Hailey cried, halting everyone midrise, their butts four inches from their chairs. Rudy and Gage frowned, but Cherry sat right back down, her expression warm and encouraging.

"I think he's wrong. Gage clearly has a strong grasp of basic marketing. And he's right. Sex Sells 101 is often an effective advertising ploy." She paused, letting the emphasis on the word ploy sink in. "But is that really what you want? A ploy? Gimmicks only go so far, don't they?"

She addressed that question to Cherry, who suddenly looked very tired. As if all this talking had sapped her energy.

"Gimmicks have their place," Cherry said, her shrug indicating that their place was nowhere near her.

At her words, the men settled back in their chairs. Gage's expression was guarded, but Rudy was watching his muse like a hawk.

That was her hook, Hailey knew. No matter how much Rudy might want to see women prancing down his runway come February wearing tiny strips of leather and stilettos, he'd defer to what Cherry wanted.

"Sex sells.... In this case, it'd sell to a very specific market. But you want to make this year's debut extraordinary, don't you, Mr. Rudolph? This is the first year you've ever built a line around a person rather than a theme."

"That's true. Although Miss Bella hasn't signed the agreement yet," Rudy said with a jovial sort of laugh that did nothing to disguise his concern over that detail.

"Once I know exactly what I'd be representing, I'll make my decision," Cherry said, her words friendly but firm, with just a hint of impatience. "My image, and my personal comfort levels, must be in sync with anything I do."

"Which is why Merry Widow is perfect for you," Hailey said, leaning forward and clasping both hands on her knees. "It's a line that focuses on the image of romance, of the ultimate in feminine empowerment, while ensuring you feel so real you can't be anything but comfortable."

Out of breath, Hailey forced herself not to grin. She was proud of herself. That'd sounded pretty awesome.

"I beg to differ," Gage broke in. His tone was smooth-as-silk friendly, but the look in his eyes was diamond hard. And, Hailey noted, just a little surprised. Obviously he really hadn't expected her to be any sort of competition. Just a bit of fluff, like her lingerie.

He turned to Cherry, charm oozing from every pore. Hailey wanted to hate that he could do that. But who could blame a man for being fabulous at what he did? She just wished he could be fabulous somewhere else.

Like in her bedroom.

"Miss Bella, you're a very sexy woman. Gorgeous, talented and not one to shy away from using both of those as a platform for your voice. Much like Milano Lingerie, you're distinctive, strong and bold. If anyone can showcase feminine appeal and edgy allure, you can."

Gage leaned closer to the torch singer, letting his smile widen, and laid a hand on the arm of her chair. He didn't touch her; he just suggested an intimacy, a connection.

Hailey had to actually clench her butt to the chair to keep herself seated. She wanted to leap out of her seat and smack his hand away.

You'd think her stomach would be too crowded already with nerves, panic and hurt to have room for one more nasty, balled-up emotion. But there it was, jealousy in all its hairy ugliness. "There is a lot to recommend both lines," Cherry said slowly, her gaze shifting back and forth between Gage and Hailey. "I'm not sure which I feel best fits my image."

"Isn't a better question, what message do you want to send by wearing the line?" Hailey asked before Gage could jump in with another one of those devastatingly effective innuendos. "Do your songs, does your image, equate to sex? Or to romance? Lingerie is about more than the physical act. It's about intimacy."

When the redhead's brows drew together as she considered that, Hailey took a deep breath and, ignoring her natural abhorrence for aggressive pushiness, plunged on.

"That's what it all comes down to, after all. Sex, which is strictly physical satisfaction. Or romance, which invokes the emotions, the mind and the imagination."

"There's plenty of imagination in sex," Gage said, finally dropping his charming facade to frown at Hailey.

"Sex sells for a very good reason. People like it. People want it. Sex, in leather lingerie, will appeal across the board to men and women alike. Fluff might get a few women's attention, but it won't get the men's."

"Women buy more lingerie," Hailey pointed out.

"To appeal to men," he countered.

"Romance sells much better than sex," she argued. "It sends a more empowering, desirable message and will bring in a wider customer base."

His hands loosely clasped between his knees, Gage leaned forward. He was still many feet away, but it was as if he'd moved right into her space. As if he were intimately pressing against her. Hailey's breath caught. Her body heated. She bit her lip, trying not to squirm and damning him for being able to trigger such intense sexual awareness in her body.

"Sex outsells romance. Just check the internet stats."

"Porn?" Hailey dismissed with a sniff.

"Pays well," he countered.

"Is that what Rudolph department stores is selling? Or are they focused on creating an exclusive image?"

"They're selling a trend." Gage's tone and expression were pure triumph. As if she'd just set him up to make the perfect point.

Hailey glared. She wanted to kick him for looking so smug over there, wearing his brilliant marketing-wizard face.

"Well, this has been a great meeting," Rudy interrupted before they could get to the eye-poking and name-calling portion of their argument. "The two of you have presented us with some very good reasons to consider either line. Both have great merit. But of course, we can only feature one."

Hailey ripped her gaze from Gage's smug, sexy grin to look at the man who could make or break her future. Suddenly she wanted to cry. She could see it, the decision on

Rudy's face. She'd got so close. She'd done her best and jumped way outside her comfort zone to argue for her designs. And he was still going to go with Milano?

She looked away, blinking fast to clear her burning eyes. The decorations lining the wall caught her eye. Awards. Trophies. Photo after photo of Rudy winning this or that. Many of them, she noted through narrowed eyes, at poker tournaments.

"Why don't we make a bet," she heard herself say.

"What?"

"I beg your pardon?"

"Ooh," Rudy intoned, rubbing his hands together and leaning forward. "What kind of bet?"

Hailey licked her lips, not having a clue what kind of bet. She tried to think over the roaring sound of panic rushing through her head. Taking calming breaths to try to overcome her horror at the temerity of challenging Rudolph. This man could break her. Wasn't leaving on good terms, with a possible order of future lingerie, enough? She'd made a good contact, and she'd garnered enough press and attention to possibly pull in more sales.

But a few sales and orders weren't going to be enough to get a loan the size she needed to save her business.

So stomach rock tight and nerves dancing, she wet her lips and forced herself to smile.

"Well, the question really comes down to which will be a stronger selling point for your spring line. Sex—" she bit off the word, letting it hang there for a second, then gave a deep sigh before adding "—or romance?"

Gage gave her an arch look as if to say, *didn't we already cover this?* Determined to get her point, whatever the hell it was, out before he interrupted and took over again, she sat up straighter and tilted her head toward Cherry.

"Miss Bella can sell either. But the true question is,

which one will have the widest appeal? Which one will send customers clamoring for the latest in Rudolph Exclusives? And," she added triumphantly, "which one will enhance Cherry's reputation and image in a way that benefits her career, as well?"

"I'm hearing the repeat of your sales pitch, but I'm not hearing a bet," Gage murmured.

"We each get two chances to prove our point. Sex or romance. Then Mr. Rudolph and Miss Bella decide which they think really offers the most to their prospective images."

"How do you propose we do that?"

She had no freaking clue.

But she wasn't going to let him know that.

Instead, Hailey fluttered her lashes and offered up a smug smile of her own.

"I have so many ideas, my challenge will be narrowing them down."

"We do have to get moving on this," Rudy started to say, his words drawn out and hesitant as he tried to read Cherry's reaction. "It can't go on for too long."

Trying not to let on how desperate she was, Hailey cast her mind around every idea, every argument, every possible persuasion she could offer that might get him to agree. She had nothing. Biting her lip, she looked at Cherry. The other woman didn't really want to parade around in a leather bikini, did she? It would probably chafe something horrible.

"I can give it a week," Cherry said, her eyes on Hailey. "At that point, I'll be able to let you know which lingerie line I prefer. And if I'm going to take your offered position as spokesmodel."

SON OF A BITCH.

Gage couldn't figure it out.

He'd been right there, in the winning position. They all knew Rudy was going to go with Milano.

That contract, and his freedom, had been in the palm of his hand. He'd felt bad, just a little, about playing to his strengths as hard as he had. Hailey was sweet, and clearly a talented designer. But she didn't have that killer edge that made the difference between success and luck.

Then, just when he was ready to pull out his pen and sign the contract, the pretty little blonde had outflanked him. Again. How the hell did she keep doing that? He didn't know if it was deliberate, or if Hailey was just lucky.

But now thanks to her, instead of heading up to Tahoe and mapping out the details of his brilliant kick-his-brother's-ass-and-prove-he-was-the-best business plan, he was going to be stuck pimping sex wrapped in leather for two weeks?

No way.

"I don't have another week available to negotiate this project," he said, shifting his body so he was facing Rudy. Not so much to cut the women out of the discussion as to keep Hailey from his line of sight. If he didn't see her, he wouldn't get distracted and she couldn't work her sweet magic. "And I thought you said you wanted your people moving on the advertising before Christmas. That means you don't have time to waste, either. It's not like they can whip up a brilliant campaign in a couple of days."

"You think this is a waste?"

Gage kept his grimace to a twitch, smoothing out his expression before he gave Cherry a warm smile. Her expression didn't budge. She was clearly a woman who expected to be catered to, which meant he'd just made a major misstep.

"I think your time is valuable, and that you must have more important things to do for the holidays than play…" He paused, then hating himself but knowing it had to be done, he gave Hailey an arch look. "What is it you wanted us to do again?"

She wet her lips, the move making the shell-pink flesh glisten. His own mouth watered.

He'd offered her an out yesterday. A chance to pick up a solid bevy of new clients, all ready to order. If she was as desperate as that look in her eyes indicated, she'd have grabbed his offer with both hands. She had to know her tiny company didn't stand much of a chance against an enterprise like Milano. He'd checked into her business this morning before the meeting and she wasn't heavily in debt or having obvious issues.

So it came down to one thing. There was only one reason she could have refused his offer and was pushing this silly bet idea.

Pure stubbornness.

"Maybe once we know how you think this bet will work, we can figure out the timeline," Rudy said, his tone pacifying. Not to Hailey, Gage knew. But to the lush, red-headed torch singer.

"Maybe we should just—"

"My thought is that Gage and I each take turns planning a scenario that we feel showcases the image our lingerie will offer. Mine would be to show you how romance would enhance both your reputation as a trendsetter and fashion icon, Mr. Rudolph, and the sensual image Miss Bella's built over the last few years, as well."

She tilted her head toward Gage, a lock of baby blond hair sliding over her cheek, reminding him of how soft it was. How it'd felt to tilt her face up to best receive his kisses.

Shake it off, man, Gage told himself, actually twitching his shoulders. *Don't let her get to you again.*

"And what do you suggest my scenario would be?"

"Whatever situation you think would best showcase the message your lingerie brings to the table, of course."

What message did leather panties suit?

A strip club? Bondage basement? Adult video store?

Hell, maybe she had a point.

From the look on her face, she knew it, too.

And so did Rudy and Cherry, Gage noted.

Crap.

"Not a problem," he lied smoothly.

"I like this idea. A lot, actually. And it'll only take a week," Cherry said with a languid wave of one hand, a walnut-sized diamond flashing in the morning light as she dismissed Gage's tight schedule. "But I've commitments, so my time is scarce. You'll have to plan these little tableaux for evenings when I'm not performing."

They all looked to Rudy, who ran one long-fingered hand over his bald head as he gauged Cherry's expression. When he saw her determined interest, he sighed and gave a shrug.

"Okay, then. Cherry performs four nights this week, if I remember correctly." At her nod, he continued. "That gives you three to choose among. Figure out the details and let us know by five this afternoon. If at any time either of you fails to create your scenario or in any way drops the ball, the contract goes to the other person."

He waited a beat, then stood, putting an end to the meeting.

Gage waited for the pleasantries to wind up and for the old man to escort Cherry from the room. The minute they hit the doorway, he turned on Hailey.

Damned if she wasn't adorable. Even through his irritation, all he could think of was how cute she was. And remember what she'd tasted like.

"Well, it looks like it's not quite over yet." Her voice was filled with bravado, but she'd chewed off her pretty pink lipstick and her eyes were wary. As if she wasn't quite sure what he was going to do now that they'd lost their buffer.

What he wanted to do was slide his hand up those smooth red tights, right under her skirt, and see if they were the kind that went to the waist or just to the top of the thighs. He wanted to touch her, to warm himself against her sweet little body again.

But mostly he wanted to tie her to his bed, where she couldn't cause him any further trouble. Except, he acknowledged as he shifted from one foot to the other, trouble to the fit of his slacks.

"You know what you've done, don't you?" he said, keeping his words quiet in hopes that the anger wouldn't come through. If the way her eyes widened as she leaned backward was any indication, he didn't succeed.

It didn't stop her from lifting her chin and giving him a so-what look, though. "I did exactly what I came here to do. I did my best to get this account."

Gage laughed. Couldn't fault her that.

"Sweetheart, you've got us double-dating."

7

How DID A girl dress for a date with her competition—the sexiest man on earth—a wealthy pervert with the power to make or break her future and a gorgeous woman who intimidated the hell out of her?

With killer lingerie, of course.

Hopefully, killer lingerie would make this evening magic. Parking her car, Hailey grimaced. Two days after she'd issued the bet challenge, and it was time to rock. She took a deep breath, the move pushing her lacy-edged breasts tight against the sheer fabric of her blouse. Tonight was all about romance. But that didn't mean romance wasn't sexy. To prove that point, she'd opted for exquisite lace and satin in a delicate shade of pink under a blouse the color of milk chocolate. Her full skirt, the same shade of brown, hit midthigh, the better to show off the delicate seams and bows climbing the backs of her sheer stockings.

That her thong and garter belt matched the pale pink bra visible through the filmy fabric of her blouse was Hailey's little secret. One that people might guess, which meant it'd titillate and intrigue. Not scream "do me because I wear sexy underwear"...like *some people's* lingerie.

"Miss North, you look amazing," the maître d' greeted as she swept into Carinos, where she'd set the scene for her special scenario pitch. It wasn't so much that she wanted to rub in Gage's face what he'd lost by choosing a contract over her. No. Carinos was her favorite restaurant. If he ate his heart out in addition to the delicious dinner she'd arranged, well, that was icing on the cake.

"Thanks, Paolo," she responded with a warm smile, following him to the private room she'd arranged, pleased at the ambience along the way. Soft music, flickering candles, the delicate scent of roses filling the air as they skirted the main dining room and stopped just short of the atrium, with its lush display of winter roses.

"The rest of the party should be along shortly," she told Paolo, slipping him a generous tip as he gestured to the door of their private room.

"One gentleman is already here, Miss North. I'll escort the others as soon as they arrive."

Figuring that gentleman was Gage trying to get the jump on her, and wanting to be sure Paolo was waiting for Rudy and Cherry, she told him she'd seat herself. Hailey took a deep breath, mentally going over her checklist for the evening, then plastered on her biggest smile as she entered the room.

Her breath stuck in her chest.

Oh, baby, Gage was gorgeous.

The navy suit fit him to perfection. And since his back was turned while he stared out the glass wall at the flower garden, she could see how well tailored the slacks were, cupping his butt in a way that made her jealous of the fabric.

Then he turned.

And the view from the front was even sexier.

Puffing out a little breath, she forced herself to lift her gaze to his face. It was like trying to heft a very reluctant elephant over her head. Her eyes wanted to slide right back down.

"Ahh, my date." His smile was wickedly teasing and

light. But his gaze turned hot fast as he took in her appearance. "You look lovely."

Uh-oh.

The first rule she'd set for this evening was to keep a distance between herself and Gage. To stay as far away as politely possible so she could maintain control. Of her thoughts. Of her body. And of the situation.

But as he crossed the room and took her hands in his, all she could do was sigh. After all, it'd be rude to pull away.

"Thank you." She gazed up at him, her fingers itching to touch his perfectly styled hair, to muss it just a little so it fell across his forehead like it had the first evening they'd met.

Then he raised one of her hands to his lips, brushing his mouth over her knuckles. Hailey's knees almost buckled. Talk about romantic. It was as if he had magic in those lips of his.

And if he could get her all weak in the knees with such a sweet move, what else could that mouth do? She knew his kisses were hot enough to melt her panties.

Suddenly she was desperate to know how much more power he had. To feel more of what he had to offer.

And he knew it.

The look in Gage's eyes was a combination of wicked amusement and sexual heat. A promise. One she had every faith he could keep, and one she was quickly becoming desperate to feel.

"Miss North…"

Hailey's eyes dropped to Gage's mouth. Those lips were curved. Soft. Full. She wanted to taste them. To feel them trailing down her body.

"Excuse me."

"Someone wants you," Gage said, his words low and amused.

Him?

"Miss North?"

Dammit.

Hailey pulled her hands, and her body, away from Gage and turned. Face on fire, she shook her head, trying to toss off the spell, then turned to give Paolo a shaky smile.

"Yes?"

"A message for you." As polite and circumspect as if he were totally oblivious to the sexual sparks flying around the room, he stepped forward and handed Hailey a slip of paper. Then, without a word, he turned smartly on one heel and exited. Leaving Hailey alone with Gage and all that sexual temptation.

Frowning, she opened the slip of paper and read it. Her frown turned into a scowl and she crushed the note in her fist.

"What's wrong?"

"Apparently Cherry can't make it. She's not feeling well this evening. She sent the message through Rudy, who said he'd meet us in an hour and to go ahead and start dinner without him."

Damn. Damn, damn, damn.

Hailey all but stomped her foot and shook her fist at the ceiling, she was so frustrated.

She'd planned this evening so carefully. The most romantic restaurant, a private room. She'd ordered the meal, the dessert, the champagne and even picked the music, all with the idea of impressing Cherry and Rudy.

Now, neither of them was here.

Her grand plan to prove she was the best pick for the contract, *poof.* Gone. She swallowed hard, trying to get past the lump of tears clogging her throat.

"Well, I guess we can get on with the evening," Gage said, his tone close to a shrug. "Rudy will get here when he gets here."

"What's the point? I'm not trying to convince *you* of the

merits of a romantic evening," she said, jerking one shoulder in a dismissive shrug. *Be nice,* a part of her chided. He might be her competition, but Gage was still a major player who knew a lot of people. If she angered him, he could easily spread the word that she was a bitch or a diva. Or just a pain in his butt.

But for once, she didn't care about that cautioning voice. She wasn't worried about upsetting anyone. Not when she was already this upset herself.

"Look, have a glass of wine and let's eat. We might as well," Gage persuaded. "There's no point in letting this ambience go to waste. The wine is chilled. The stomachs are growling. Let's enjoy it."

Hailey looked around the room.

Ambience, indeed. A cozy table for four covered in white linen, lit candles amid holiday greenery on the table and the sideboard. Instead of the Christmas tunes that were playing gently out in the restaurant, the speakers here played the bluesy romantic tones of Cherry's music. A bottle of wine waited, as did a tray of hors d'oeuvres and fruit.

And Gage.

Looking oh so sexy and sympathetic.

She might be able to resist the sexy—and that was a huge *might*—but the sympathy in his dark eyes? Her heart melted a little; it was so unused to anyone seeming to give two good damns about her.

"Maybe we should hold the meal until Rudy joins us," she murmured, sure an evening alone with Gage was a bad idea. One that'd feel amazingly good, but still… "Wouldn't it be better to wait for him?"

"No." Gage took her hand, led her to a seat with a perfect view of the garden and held out the chair. "He said to start without him. I'm starving, so let's eat."

Hailey hesitated, then sat. Because she was starving. Not because she wanted more time with Gage. She'd been so amped over this evening, so busy planning it all, that she hadn't eaten a thing since breakfast.

"This doesn't count as my pitch for the contract. Once we eat or drink, unless Rudy or Cherry are here, the pitch is void." Determined to settle that point, Hailey gave him an intent, narrow-eyed look. "Okay?"

"You sure?" Gage leaned back in his chair, giving her a considering look that made her shiver and wish she'd worn something that didn't actually show her underwear. When she nodded, he lifted his glass of ice water with a twist of lemon and drank. "I guess we'll just have to call this a date, then."

Her eyes rounding, Hailey gulped.

"No—"

"Hey, you said it," he interrupted. "It's not for business. Which means this is a date. Just you and me and what dates are all about. Pure pleasure."

GAGE LOVED WATCHING Hailey's face. She was an open book, every emotion, every thought playing across those pretty features. Right now, her slick berry lips pursed and her brows creased, he read irritation, dismay and—yes, oh yes, baby—a whole lot of interest and sexual heat.

He figured the heated interest was enough to overcome the other dismay. And he kinda liked the irritation. It meant he was keeping her on edge. And Hailey on edge was fun. Like watching a hissing, spitting kitten.

"This is not a date."

Gage grinned. She was so cute when she was stubborn.

"Sure it is. You. Me. Candlelight dinner, all the foofy romantic accompaniments. That says date."

"Foofy?" Her green eyes slitted and she spat the word, just like the hissing kitten he'd thought her. "You call romance *foofy*?"

"Sure. It's like frosting." When she frowned and shook

her head, he elaborated. "Frosting is sweet. It's fluffy and tasty and quite often decadent. But it's not the point. The point is the cake."

"And you think leather lingerie is cake?"

"No." He waited for the stiffness to drain from her shoulders and her face to relax again before adding, "The cake is sex."

He laughed when she almost fumbled her glass of water.

"You're awfully naive for a woman who designs sex clothes."

"I don't design sex clothes. I design lingerie. Underwear, sleepwear, apparel to make a woman feel confident and attractive and empowered."

As much as he was enjoying the view of her face, those round cheeks flushed and her eyes flashing, Gage let his gaze drop.

Her see-through blouse was ruffly and full, creating a hazy distraction from the delicious curve of her breasts, highlighted to perfection in a pink bra. He had to hand it to her. Lacy and dotted with pearly things, the bra was attractive. And if it made her feel confident and empowered, well, more power to that sweet satin.

But he was thinking sex when he looked at it.

A fact he knew was clear on his face when he met her eyes again. A fact that, if the way her gaze blurred and her breath hitched were any indication, got her a little excited.

Good. He still had hope of rescuing this evening. As irritated as he was to put off his departure to Tahoe until next week after he'd nailed down winning this contract, spending more time with Hailey was a pretty good consolation.

He'd be even happier if they could spend some of that time naked. Or at least—his gaze dropped again—seeing her lingerie in more detail.

"Then I guess I'm all for empowerment if it comes in

pink satin and—" He made a show of leaning closer. "Is that lace tan or brown?"

Pink, even darker than the last blush, washed her cheeks. Gage grinned. Teasing her was fun. Something he'd never actually experienced when it came to business. Missing was that sharp competitive edge, the driving need to win. Not that he had any doubt he'd triumph when it came to the contract. But for once, it was more about enjoying himself than proving himself.

Just then, the waiter stepped in with wine and a tray.

Gage leaned back, watching Hailey relax as she chatted with the man as he poured wine, letting him know it'd just be the two of them for dinner so to go ahead and serve. He waited until the man had left before arching a brow.

"We don't order for ourselves?"

She gave an impatient little sniff, then after an internal debate that had him wondering what she was hiding, she shrugged.

"The point of this dinner is romance. Which is more than just candles, wine and music."

"I might hate whatever you chose, though," he teased.

"If you do, then I'm not very good at relaying the message of romance, am I?"

She said it as if romance was real. As if it was more than a sales pitch. He knew she was sweet, bordering on naive. But to really believe in that fairy tale? She wasn't crazy.

"C'mon," Gage said with a laugh. "It's just us. Be honest. You're not really buying into this whole romance-versus-sex thing, are you? That's only a ploy to strengthen your pitch."

Her lower lip stuck out when she frowned. He wanted to reach over and trace the pad of his thumb against it, test its softness.

"You don't believe in romance?"

"It's a device. A sales pitch." He waved one hand to indicate the room, lifting his glass of wine with the other. "It's all imagery."

He sipped his wine, then gave an approving nod, pretending she wasn't staring at him as though he'd spouted a third head and started babbling about the coming of aliens to take over the world and dress everyone in little pink tutus.

"Imagery? Romance is emotions, not packaging."

"What's its purpose?" he challenged, leaning back to rest one arm on the back of his chair and giving her a curious look. "To sell something, right? Sex, maybe? Companionship? Accoutrements like candles and wine and lingerie?"

Instead of rising to the bait and defending the fluff and froth of romance as he'd expected, Hailey just stared. Her look was intense, searching. Gage shifted, wondering if she could suddenly see through him the way he could see through her blouse. If so, he was pretty sure she wasn't nearly as intrigued by what she saw.

"Is your lingerie just packaging?" she countered. "Is it just a way to make money?"

Yeah.

That was how his grandfather had built the company. On the concept of seeing what people thought they wanted and coming up with ideas to meet those wants.

That was how Devon developed new product offerings. He looked at the ideas people thought were so appealing and made them better. Bigger. More attractive, so they'd pay top dollar.

And that was how Gage sold it. By tapping into what people thought they needed and convincing them that his product was the only one that could perfectly meet that need.

It was Psychology 101, combined with Economics and Marketing 102.

But he didn't think telling her that was going to score him any points.

So he shrugged, then shot a smile at the waiter, who chose that perfect moment to bring their food.

"Imagery is imagination, yes. It's packaging and appeal. But romance is more than that," she said as their dishes were set in front of them. His favorite spinach salad, he noted with a frown. "Romance is emotions."

"Imagery taps into the emotions. Plays them," he said, still frowning at the salad and wondering how she knew exactly what he liked. He glanced up to ask her and winced at the look on her face. Clearly she didn't think the emotions were something to be played with.

He waited for her to chew him out.

Instead, she leaned closer, resting one hand on his forearm for support as she lifted her mouth toward his ear.

"And just so you know," she said, her words a whisper of heat against the side of his head, low enough so the waiter couldn't hear, "the lace is bittersweet chocolate. You know, like frosting."

Gage closed his eyes and bit back a groan.

Every time he thought he had the upper hand, she found a way to knock him off balance.

"Enjoy," the waiter said, breaking his thoughts.

Opening his eyes, Gage watched the guy leave. In the three seconds it took him to regain his equilibrium, Hailey dug into her own salad with a tiny moan of delight.

"I'm so glad you insisted we eat," she admitted with a sheepish smile. "I was starving."

"What's for dessert?" he asked, noting that her salad was slightly different from his. Spinach, yes, but hers had strawberries, which he was allergic to. Did she know that? "Something frosted, I hope."

She laughed, looking more relaxed than he'd seen her since they'd realized they were rivals.

"You don't really mean that about romance, do you? That you don't think it's real?" she asked after a few bites. "I didn't peg you as the kind of guy who didn't believe in the softer side of love."

Another one for the imagery books. Gage shoved a forkful of spinach in his mouth to keep that opinion to himself.

"I think we buy into what we want to believe," he finally said. "If you want to believe that love is romantic, you look for that. If someone else thinks that sex is about physical gratification, they find images to support that belief."

"And if I wanted to believe you're a grumpy sort of emotional curmudgeon who, after being exposed to a little romance, has his heart grow three times too large, will I see that, too?" she teased, her smile bright and her eyes dancing as she referenced his Grinch costume.

"I have no doubt you could make something grow three times larger...." It was difficult, but he managed to hold back his smile until he saw that pink on her cheeks. "But I doubt it'd involve my heart. Disappointed?"

Her lips pursed, as if she was debating.

"Well, I suppose it won't jeopardize my chances of winning the account to admit that I was disappointed to find out you were my competition," she said with a little shrug. The move did delicious things under that filmy shirt, the lush pillows of her breasts moving against the satin bra as if protesting their confinement. Gage's fingers ached to touch. To see if she was as soft as she looked.

"Disappointed because you are worried I'll win?" he asked, too distracted by the view to worry about nicing up his words.

"Disappointed that it meant we can't date," she denied, just a hint of irritation. "The man I met at the party was very appealing."

It wasn't her words, so much as the snap in her tone

that grabbed his attention. Gage noted the annoyance as it flashed in her eyes, then was gone.

"But now you're wondering if that man was real." Gage frowned, wondering that, too. And wondering why he cared so much.

"You're obviously real, seeing as you're sitting right next to me all but licking—" she hesitated, took a breath that made her breasts shift deliciously again, then said archly "—your plate. The only question I have is who you really are."

Marcus Milano's son.

Devon Milano's younger brother.

The last one consulted, the one who least fit the Milano mold.

And—definitely—a man who didn't need a pretty little blonde poking into who he *really* was.

Time to change the subject.

"Isn't the more important question how you're going to pitch this romantic fluff idea of yours?" he said with just a hint of disdain. As he'd hoped, her eyes flashed and she shifted her shoulders back into combat position.

Good.

The only time he wanted her focused on him was if it included naked skin, hot tongues and the buildup to incredible orgasms.

"You're very dismissive of something you don't understand." She arched one brow, poking a strawberry with her fork and lifting it to her mouth. She didn't bite it, though. Instead, she slid the juicy fruit over her lower lip. Gage's eyes narrowed and his body stiffened.

She smiled, her look pure triumph, as if her x-ray eyes saw through the table at his burgeoning boner.

"Don't you think you're proving my point?" Gage asked, shifting in his chair. He wasn't embarrassed at his physical reaction. But he wasn't sure where she was going with this, either. Hailey had a way of leading things along, all innocent-like, then just when he was sure he'd won, she'd bat those lashes and outmaneuver him.

He had to admire that about her.

"No." She touched the strawberry with the tip of her tongue, as if testing its taste. Gage's brain shut down and he suddenly didn't give a damn whether she won or not. Just as long as she did that same move on a particular part of his body.

"Your point was that it's just about sex. That the physical act and gratification are all that matters. My point is that the packaging is what makes that act so powerful. The buildup, the anticipation. The emotional journey."

She paused to let her words sink in, then bit that strawberry right in half. Gage almost groaned out loud as his dick did a happy leap to full attention.

"You know," she reminded him softly as she licked a tiny piece of strawberry off her lip. "The romance."

"Visuals," he countered after clearing his throat. Then, always ready to play to win, he leaned closer. Close enough to get in her space. Close enough that the delicate scent of her perfume wrapped around him. And close enough to see the rapid beat of her pulse against her throat.

"Imagery is powerful. I could describe to you exactly how I want to strip those clothes from your body, what I'd like to do once you're naked and beneath me, how I want to taste you and where I'll touch." He waited, letting those words sink in. And sink they did, as she dropped her fork next to her plate and blinked quickly, looking as if she was trying to fan away that image with her eyelashes. Gage grinned. "But that's sex. Which is my point."

As if he'd been waiting around the corner for just the right moment, the waiter came in again with their entrées. Gage vowed to give the guy an extra tip for perfect timing, since Hailey now had to sit quietly, looking shell-shocked and absorbing his words instead of skipping right past them while trying to prove her point.

A point, Gage had to admit as his dinner was slid in front of him, that was pretty solid. If she was basing romance on good food and ambience, she'd have nailed it. He looked closer at the plate, noting all his favorites, from the way the steak was cooked to the type of vegetables.

"So what'd you do? Hire an investigator to scope out what I eat? If Cherry and Rudy were here, would they be having the same?"

"If Cherry and Rudy were here, their meals would fit their tastes," she said primly, cutting a delicate sliver off her chicken.

Gage glanced at the place settings, trying to see how she'd designated it so the waiter knew who got what. They all looked the same. And he'd chosen his own seat, and hers, so that wasn't it.

"Clever, but I don't see what makes the meal choice romantic. Or what it has to do with lingerie," he added, needing to remember the real purpose of this evening.

"No?" She gave him one of those looks only women could pull off. The kind that made it clear she wondered where he kept his brains but didn't hold his lack of knowledge against him since he was so damned cute. "Romance is the effort to show you care about someone else's preferences. It's putting in a little extra time to make sure they feel appreciated. Special."

"My grandma does that. Is she romancing me?"

"Does she do it in a private room by candlelight, with your favorite music in the background?"

Well, there was an image. Gage grimaced as it filled his head. Damn. She kept winning those points.

Time to turn the tables.

"So tell me, what's the point of all this romance stuff

you're so hot on?" He disguised his shift closer to her chair by filling her wineglass. "Isn't the end result the same?"

"The result?"

"When a guy romances a girl, or vice versa, the hoped-for result is sex, isn't it? Same as a woman wearing lingerie. She wears it to get—" Gage winced before a very unromantic phrase slipped from his lips and corrected "—attention. The kind that will lead to sex."

"When you're hungry, do you prefer filet mignon or a burger from the convenience store?"

Ouch.

"Then I suppose Milano Lingerie's place in that scenario would be, what? The equivalent to hunting down your own meal in the jungle and roasting it over an open fire?"

Her lips twitched and delight danced in her eyes, but Hailey shook her head.

"Oh, no. Milano's not *that* adventurous. Maybe a gourmet-catered, rich-boy frat party," she mused, tapping her finger to her chin in a way that was both adorable and amusing.

Gage laughed. She was fun. Not just fun in a cute-to-tease-and-see-her-blush kind of way. But clever. Smart and talented. Add that to a hot body and a gorgeous face, and she was trouble.

A smart man took on trouble only when he had time to deal with it. Gage had no time right now. He had a goal, a plan for his life. He didn't have time to enjoy the kind of trouble Hailey represented.

But he had a point to prove.

With that in mind, he held her gaze with his and let his smile drop. His look became intense, hot. Sexual. He let her see how attracted he was. Clear on his face, he knew, was everything he wanted to do to her, with her and for her.

Hailey's smile faded. Her eyes widened and her breath quickened. Good. She was getting the message.

"Oh, I don't know. I think this Milano can be plenty adventurous," he said quietly as he leaned in closer.

He reached under the heavy cloth covering the table and touched her knee. The soft fabric of her skirt slid temptingly between his fingers and her skin. Her eyes softened, heated. Like green glass melting into passion.

He slipped his hand under her skirt, smoothing his palm up her thigh. Delighting in the silken texture of her stocking. When he reached the top of her thigh he found lace. A band of it, separating the smooth texture of her stockings and the warm silk of her skin.

"You shouldn't…" Her words trailed off into a soft, breathy sigh as he traced the lacy edge of her stockings, slipping one finger under the smooth satin garter, then skimming it between the stocking and her warm flesh.

She was so soft.

"I think I should." He pressed the flat of his palm to her thigh, his fingers now wedged between her legs. His eyes locked on hers, silently demanding she give him room.

Her lips parted, wet and glistening, and a tiny furrow creased her brow. But slowly, so slow he wanted to groan, she unclenched her thighs and let them slide apart. Just a little. So the fit was tight.

Good.

He liked tight.

8

GAGE WAS PRETTY sure he'd just found the gates of heaven. He pressed his hand higher, rubbed his thumb over the fabric covering Hailey's heated core. It was silk, like her skin.

"What color are your panties?" he asked, not bothering to clear the husky passion from his voice.

Her eyes darted to the doorway, then back to his. She bit her bottom lip. He wanted to soothe the soft pink flesh, but his hand was busy. Instead, he arched an insistent brow.

"Pink," she whispered. "Pink like my bra. The lace is chocolate."

"Yum."

He slipped his fingers beneath the hem of those pink-and-chocolate panties. He ran his index finger along the swollen flesh he found, then gently pinched.

Squirming, she gasped. But she didn't pull away.

He shifted, so to anyone walking in they simply looked as though they were in conversation. But the move put him at a better angle, so he could use his thumb to caress her clitoris while slipping one finger into her tight, sweet core.

She whimpered.

But didn't pull away.

"I can't see a thing," he murmured, his words husky thanks to the passion clogging his throat. He had to swallow before continuing. "But I can imagine what you look like under the table. Pale flesh, blond curls. I can feel how wet you are. The images are clear in my mind. Vivid. Mouthwatering."

She opened her mouth, whether to respond or not he didn't know, because all that she offered was a low, breathy moan.

He moved two fingers in, swirling and plunging in time with his thumb's rhythm on her clit.

"I can imagine what it looks like as I touch you. My mind is painting a picture of you, naked, beneath me. Of your body straining toward mine, opening wide. Welcoming."

Her breath was coming in gasps now, even as she bit her lip as if to hold back her cries.

"Now, that's an image," he said, forcing the words out as his eyes devoured her face.

She was so damned beautiful. The flush of passion washed over her delicate skin. Her eyes glazed, lids lowered but never moving from his. Her mouth.

Oh, God, her mouth.

He wanted those lips on him.

His fingers plunged deeper. He shifted angles, pressing tight along the front wall of her core.

She tightened around him. And then, one more swirling stab of his fingers, and she went over.

God, that felt good.

A satisfaction that had nothing to do with physical release poured through Gage.

He watched her explode. Her breath came in tiny pants as her body came in tiny tremors.

Unable to resist, he leaned in to take her mouth. To taste her gasps of delight. It was as if he was a part of her orgasm. As if he was deeply embedded in the passion that engulfed her. A part of her.

It was incredible.

Then all hell broke out.

Bursting their peaceful, romantic bubble was a clash of sounds. A braying laugh. A sibilant giggle. And the sound of someone asking directions to Hailey's private room. And footsteps, clomping and rat-a-tat-tatting across the atrium's cement floor.

It was like being doused with a vat of ice water while being awoken from a very hot, wet dream by a brass band. A grade-school band, at that; one that hadn't learned all the notes.

Trying to shake off the discordant horror spinning down his spine, Gage pulled his mouth off Hailey's.

The sound came closer, in all its irritating glory.

His fingers still buried in her warmth, Gage steeled himself, gritted his teeth, then looked toward the commotion just as Rudy Rudolph swept into the room. Hanging on him like a glittering party favor was a redheaded piece of fluff who, at first glance, bore a striking resemblance to Cherry.

Gage blinked away the haze of passion from his eyes and realized the only thing the woman had in common with the torch singer was their hair color and bust size.

And Rudy's interest.

"Sorry, sorry I'm late. Candy and I got caught up at a party. You know how that goes. But I'm here now."

Indeed, he was. Thank God for the man's noisy entrance and exquisite timing. A minute earlier, and Hailey would have been midorgasm. Three minutes later, and Gage was pretty sure he'd have been sliding into her hot, wet depths.

Still, it was hard to find an attitude of gratitude when his rock-hard dick was pressing painfully against his zipper.

He slid a sideways glance at Hailey. Horror was starting to replace shock on her face. Both of which had quickly chased away that glow of desire he'd enjoyed so much.

It was as much for that, as for the fact that he had to

surreptitiously move his hand back to his own lap now, that Gage cursed Rudy.

Not that the other guy cared.

His grin as oblivious as the vacant expression in his date's eyes, the old man plopped himself into the chair opposite Gage and Hailey and threw both hands wide.

"Well? Show me some romance."

HE'D GOT HER off over dinner.

In a restaurant.

With just his fingers. And his words.

Her face was still on fire. Hailey's breath caught in her chest and she had to close her eyes against the power of that memory. His murmured suggestions echoed in her mind, making her want to squirm.

Oh, yeah, those had been some powerful words.

And then, just as she'd been ready to throw off her clothes and ride him at the dinner table, her potential boss had come in.

And Gage, damn him, had acted as if nothing at all had happened. As if he hadn't had his fingers inside her as he greeted the other man. As if she hadn't been dripping wet, hot and horny beneath his hand while Rudy Rudolph introduced his bimbo du jour. Then, while Hailey was still reeling—she didn't even know if she'd said hello—he'd claimed they were finished with dinner and suggested they leave immediately for his sexy scenario.

And she'd been too busy trying to climb out of the orgasm haze to even protest.

It was enough to make a girl scream.

And not in a good way.

"Here we are," Gage said, his words just background noise to her whirlwind of thoughts. Throughout the car ride, she'd heard him chatting with Rudy and the redhead, who were in the backseat. But she hadn't taken in a word.

The most she'd been able to do was state that her pitch would take place at another time. Just as well, since she wasn't sure she'd even get her name right at this point, let alone be able to present her argument for romantic lingerie.

Still lost in thought, she absently took Gage's hand as he helped her from the passenger seat of his car. He'd insisted on driving her to *part two* of their evening. She'd tried to disagree, desperately wanting her own car—and some time to herself. But once Rudy and Candy had decided to ride along, she'd figured it was better to just go with the flow.

Now, staring up at the building in front of them while the valet took Gage's BMW, she desperately wished she'd stood up for her choice and had a car to escape with.

Pussy's Galore, the neon sign screamed in bright orange.

"Are you sure this is how you wanted to pitch your argument for Milano designs?" she asked as they approached the rough-stone building. The red light flashing over the door spelled out clearly what kind of entertainment the Pussy Cats would be providing.

And it wasn't anything Hailey wanted to see.

"I'm sure." Gage stopped, one hand on the brass door pull, and gave her an amused look. "You're not backing out, are you? Afraid of a little adventure?"

She figured her desire to hiss and scratch could be blamed on the club he was about to drag her into. But her reaction—a nervous knot in her stomach and a feeling of nausea clogged in her throat—was definitely fear.

She slid a sideways glance at Rudy, who was pretending to read the encased poster showcasing the evening's entertainment. From the smile playing over his thin lips, he thought she was afraid, too.

His date, Hailey noted, was busy checking her manicure and clearly didn't care.

Logically, Hailey knew she could object to visiting a club called Pussy's Galore. There was nothing wrong with that. It wasn't as if she was a prude or uptight in any way. Hell, she'd just had an orgasm with her chicken piccata.

She really didn't want to go into a place that screamed sex. If a romantic setting with Gage inspired an under-the-table orgasm, who knew what inhibitions she'd toss aside in a sex club.

But she didn't want to be the one who ruined the evening, either. Nor did she want to be the one going home alone by taxi while the others had fun, with Gage charming Rudy into the contract over naked bodies.

"You're paying my entry fee, I hope," she finally said, giving Gage a sassy look. "After all, I paid for dinner."

"You made this sweet girl pay for the meal?" Rudy interrupted, pulled out of his fake perusal to frown at Gage. "That's not right."

"Romance is genderless, Mr. Rudolph," Hailey said with a shrug that conveyed she didn't play to the double standard. "And it was my point for the bet, so it's only fair that I paid. Of course, that means Gage should pay for anything we encounter in here, too."

She sure hoped the going rate for hookers was a lot more than chicken.

Ten minutes later, her wrist stamped with a go-go boot and her butt perched on a magenta fur-covered chrome stool, Hailey gave Gage an arch look.

"You said it was a house of ill repute when we pulled up." At least, that was what she thought he'd said. She'd been too busy reveling in the memory of what his fingers had done between her thighs to be sure.

"Prostitution is illegal in San Francisco," he pointed out with a grin. "This is a Kitty Cat Club. More upscale and diverse than a standard strip club. There are strippers on three stages, but there's also pole dancing, a dance floor upstairs and, in case you get any ideas, a few rooms to rent by the hour in back."

She wanted to roll her eyes and blithely dismiss the innuendo. Except her thighs were still tingling from his fingers, her panties were damp from the orgasm and, thanks to the image he'd built in her head of licking her, she didn't think her nipples were ever going to lose their rock-hard perkiness.

So instead of being hypocritical, she opted to change the subject.

"Where did Rudy and Candy go?" She'd stepped into the bathroom after they'd entered the club and hadn't seen the odd couple since.

"I'm not sure. He said something about getting drinks, and that he'd catch up with us in a minute." Gage glanced toward the back with a frown. "But he headed in the opposite direction from the bar."

She followed his gaze toward the bank of doors along the back wall, all with lights over the top, a few lit bright red to show they were occupied.

"You don't think…"

"You don't not think…" he countered, his scowl deepening. Hailey didn't figure this was the moment to point out that since Rudy was here, this did count as one of Gage's scenarios. Then she frowned, too. What if Rudy's little private party was the kind of thing that proved Gage right, that it really was only sex that mattered?

Nope, she told herself. Not going to think about that. Rudy was the pervy, have-sex-anywhere-and-everywhere-while-he-could-still-get-it-up kind of guy. This was probably just business as usual for him.

Still… Her frown deepened. It did count as one of Gage's scenarios. And maybe a successful one, at that.

"So you come here often?" she asked, wanting to distract both of them from the image of that skinny, old, bald man and whatever he was doing in the room with the red light.

"Do I look like the kind of guy who spends a lot of time at a place called Pussy's Galore?" he asked, looking a little insulted.

"Well, you don't exactly seem like the kind of guy who had to do a lot of research to come up with what scenario you thought would best prove your point about sexy lingerie." As if to echo Hailey's words, a waitress wearing a tiny blue teddy, stockings and six-inch Lucite heels approached them with a pitcher and four glasses.

"Pussycat punch," she said, setting the tray on the table between them, then poured them each a glass of the neon-pink liquid. "Your tasty treats will be out in just a second, Gage."

"Thanks, Mona."

Mona? Hailey pressed her lips together but couldn't hold back her laugh. Eyes wide and trying to look innocent, she met Gage's glare with a shrug.

"What? It's not like the reserved sign meant that this is your very own special table or that the waitress, who knows you by name, asked about your family. I believe you when you say you don't come here all the time. I really do."

His scowl deepened.

"She just might ask that of everyone," he muttered. He looked so abashed, if he'd been standing he'd have his toe scuffing the floor. Hailey told herself not to melt, but man, he was so cute.

"She'd ask about your family?" she clarified.

When he nodded, the giggles escaped like champagne bubbles. She couldn't help it.

"Look, my brother is one of the investors in this club. He's big on keeping on top of his investments and I've come in with him from time to time to check up on things."

"Of course. That makes perfect sense." Her thoughts

putting an end to the laughter, Hailey put on a serious face and nodded. "I'm sure you only visit for the articles, view the women as hardworking employees and never, ever enjoy yourself."

He shrugged.

"I did try to pole dance once." He gave her a teasing look. "You do know what pole dancing is, right?"

He said it as if she were a complete innocent. What? Wasn't it enough that she designed lingerie—a product that by its very nature demanded an awareness of sex? How did that get her a ticket to the purity princess hall of fame?

Hell, she'd just let him feel her up, and bring her down, in a restaurant on what was questionably their first date.

And he still looked at her as if she were a sweet little thing who'd run screaming at the sight of a fully erect penis.

Hailey's shoulders stiffened and her chin lifted. Was it because she was a proponent of romance? Was that why he kept dismissing her sexual savvy?

She should ignore it. She didn't have anything to prove.

But dammit, the man made her think silk scarves, whipped cream and doing it doggy style. She'd be damned if he'd dismiss her as unworthy of those thoughts.

"Let's see, pole dancing," she mused, tapping one finger on her lower lip. "Crazy gymnastic moves that require an incredible amount of upper body and core strength in order to climb a hard, phallic-shaped dance partner."

She waited for that to sink in, then leaned closer. Close enough to breathe in the scent of his soap. Close enough to see his pupils dilate and his gaze fog as the image played through his mind.

"There's something so empowering about grabbing hold of that big, hard pole and sliding yourself up and down its length." Her gaze locked on his, she pulled her glass of pussycat punch toward her and wrapped her lips around the straw. She waited just a second, watching his pulse jump in his throat, then sucked. Hard.

And that's how it's done, she thought with a grin when Gage closed his eyes and gave a soft groan. That'd show him not to dismiss her as a naive good girl.

"You've pole danced?" he clarified when he opened his eyes again, looking at her as if he wanted to cement that visual in his brain. "In a skimpy outfit?"

Hailey's lips twitched and she took another sip of the surprisingly delicious punch.

"All the way to the top. In short shorts and a cropped T-shirt," she confirmed. He didn't need to know it'd been in a gym with fourteen other women during an exercise class. Why ruin the romance or, to use his term, the image.

"They have poles in the back for customer use. Let's go." He was off his stool, his fingers around her wrist before Hailey could swallow her punch.

Freaked, she started to shake her head. It was one thing to claim she'd danced the pole. It was another to do it in front of him.

"I don't think so," she started to say.

Before she could launch her full protest—or even come up with how to do it without making him look at her like a Pollyanna again—their waitress returned with a tray covered with snack bowls. Hailey squinted. Was that cat food?

Before she could use it as a distraction to keep Gage from trying to introduce her to a dancing pole, Rudy came strutting across the room, weaving between people like a happy rooster. Hailey didn't wonder at his smile, given that he was followed by a very disheveled Candy, who was hand in hand with another woman.

"Three of them?" she murmured, a little awed.

"Gotta hand it to the guy. He's not shy about having a good time," Gage muttered back, shaking his head.

Hailey wrinkled her nose.

"I'll bet you think this proves your point." It was all she could do not to slip right into a pout. Why couldn't Cherry have felt well tonight? If she'd been here, Rudy wouldn't have gone off to get off. He'd have stayed to woo his potential spokesmodel, giving Hailey plenty of opportunity to pitch charming point after charming point.

But *nooooo*. Instead, she'd said maybe a dozen words to the guy and paid a couple hundred dollars for dinner. With nothing to show for it but an orgasm.

Albeit a freaking awesome orgasm.

"I don't know if it proves my point," Gage mused. "But it definitely proves the old man has stamina."

Yeah. That was what he had. Stamina.

And a contract that Hailey wanted.

Which was why she kept to herself her irritation at Rudy's eccentric—which sounded better than *rude, inconsiderate* and *self-indulgent*—behavior and everything else about this evening all going to hell.

But now they could finally get to the business portion of the night, which was the actual point behind all this craziness. Hailey straightened her shoulders and put on her best smile. The one that didn't show how creeped out she was at imagining a skinny man in his seventies with two women who'd have to show ID to purchase alcohol, all doing sexual gymnastics in a room that looked about the size of Hailey's shoe closet.

"Rudy," she greeted when he drew closer. "Can I pour you some punch? It's delicious."

For the first time since she'd met him, the older man looked his age. Instead of bouncing on the balls of his feet, he was dragging them. His eyes were sleepy and his shoulders drooped. But his smile… Well, that was one satisfied smile.

"Gage, Hailey, this was great. Thanks to you both, I've

discovered a new restaurant and a club. But I'm tuckered out for the night, so we'll have to talk business later."

"But we're supposed to be pitching our points," she protested.

"Just one drink?" Gage suggested, who, unlike her, sounded perfectly content to write the evening off as a pitch-fail.

"No, no. It's my bedtime. We'll meet tomorrow, though. You both still have two shots to convince me. Sound fair?"

Not bothering to wait for a response, he wrapped one arm around Candy, offered his other to the blonde, gave them all a wink and headed for the door.

Hailey was pretty sure her mouth was hanging open.

So much for stamina.

BUSINESS-WISE, Gage was calling this evening a total bust.

He'd set out with the intention of intimidating Hailey, charming Cherry and tossing enough sexual entertainment at Rudy that the guy didn't give this whole stupid bet thing any attention.

He'd ended up fascinated by Hailey, Cherry was a no-show and Rudy had just walked out with way more entertainment than Gage had figured on. And not one single thing had been accomplished toward the goal of being in Tahoe by the weekend.

"Damn," he muttered, dropping back onto the fur-covered stool.

"I'm sorry."

He gave Hailey a skeptical look. "Yeah? Really?"

"Yeah, really," she said, sincerity clear in those huge eyes. "It's not fun making big plans and putting everything you've got into a pitch and then having it fall apart."

Right. Because her scenario had fallen apart, too. Even though this evening had been a bust, he supposed he'd got the better end of the deal in pitching. At least Rudy had shown up for his and had enjoyed it enough that he'd remember the next day.

Her frown ferocious, like a kitten showing its claws, Hailey glared at the exit, then huffed a heavy sigh. Lifting the punch pitcher, she gestured to his glass. When Gage shook his head, she shrugged and refilled her own.

He should probably warn her that the sweet drink was eighty proof under all that sugar. Before he could, though, she drained it. The whole thing, in one swallow.

His body stirred, sexual interest once again beat out his irritation.

"Look," she said, gesturing with both hands as if to indicate that he observe, like, everything around her head. "I want this done, too. Until it is, my future is on hold."

"I'd have thought you'd want to drag it out. Put off the end until you'd got a side deal or other options." He knew it was a rude assessment, but dammit, she was right. He wanted this over with.

"Why would I want to drag this out? I have a life of my own, a business to run and Christmas is only a couple weeks away. Believe it or not, I have other things to do than hang out with an old man, his treat du jour and a no-show torch singer."

He noticed she hadn't mentioned him on that list. Because she didn't have better things to do than spend time with him? Or because she didn't see him as a major factor in her life.

"You're really looking forward to the deal being struck? Once it is, the options are done for making side deals, you know."

And she'd have no reason to spend time with him. He couldn't imagine a woman wanting to date the guy who'd beat her out of a seven-figure contract.

Date? Where the hell had that come from? He wasn't a dating kind of guy. He was a fun-for-a-night guy. Maybe-a-weekend-if-the-woman-was-wild kind of guy. But his life was business, his focus success. Women, except on a very temporary basis, didn't factor in.

And now he was thinking dating? Gage eyed the punch, wondering if the alcohol fumes were getting to him. Because he didn't think these kind of thoughts about women. Ever.

"Well, sure I'm looking forward to it. Because I'm going to win the deal."

Gage laughed and shook his head in admiration. She never gave up, did she?

"You don't really believe that, do you?" He gestured to the rooms at the back where Rudy had had his fun. "You think you made a more persuasive argument than I did tonight?"

"Maybe not a more persuasive argument, given that neither of the judges was there to enjoy it. But I do think I'll win in the long run."

"You're quite the idealist."

She shrugged, either ignoring his sarcasm or floating on too much punch to recognize it.

"I figured out pretty young that things rarely turn out the way I want right away. But if I work at them, if I push and try my hardest, eventually it all comes together."

She was fascinating. A mix of naïveté, faith, sexual moxie and determination. Throw in a gorgeous smile, her hot little body and a hell of a lot of talent, and that was one potent package. Still…she wasn't going to win.

"Are you thinking that law-of-attraction mumbo jumbo is going to help you somehow?" he asked.

"Nope. Simple optimism. I just keep believing until what I believe is real."

"And that works?"

Her smile dimmed for a second, then Hailey shrugged. "Sometimes it has. I'm still waiting for the others."

"Like?"

If that wasn't a nosy question, he didn't know what was. But he'd had his hand up her skirt already tonight. Why balk at poking into her private life, too.

"Like, you know, business stuff. I have this secretary. She's aces at her job, she's loyal to the company and she works magic with numbers. But she wishes I'd disappear."

Gage could relate. Plenty of people wished he'd disappear. But none of them had the nerve to show it to his face.

"Why'd you hire her?"

"She came with the company." Hailey waved her hand again, as if dismissing question-and-answer period, clearly wanting to make her point. "But here's the thing. Every month, every week. Every. Day," she said with extra emphasis. "She's getting closer to accepting me. To liking me. Now, would I have liked that approval and being included? Yes. Did I want to be remembered, maybe treated like I mattered every once in a while? Sure. But does it stop me from believing that I belong? That I'm important and special? Hell, no."

She pounded her fist on the table in emphasis. Gage quickly grabbed the glasses that were in sudden danger of toppling to the floor.

Frowning, he peered at her. He didn't know who they were talking about now, but he was sure it wasn't her secretary.

Another man?

A vicious clawing sort of fury gripped his guts. It took him a few seconds to realize the feeling was jealousy.

He didn't like it.

"But hey, I figure someday, she's going to adore me. Because, you know, I'm adorable," Hailey added, giggling and looking just as adorable as she claimed. And, he noted, looking as though the punch was having its effect.

He should take her home.

But first…

"When do you give up?"

Her frown was the tiniest furrow between her brows, as if that wasn't a question she let herself consider.

"If it's important, you don't give up."

"Isn't it smarter to check your ROI, and if the return isn't worth the investment, simply walk away? Quit expending energy." Gage shook his head, unable to imagine trying over and over again without success. Or only eking a few inches of success out of any given deal. He was an everything-or-nothing kind of guy, though.

"Isn't it smarter to do what you love, and believe that it's going to work out exactly how you want, than to give up on a dream and settle for less?" she countered.

Gage wanted to rub his gut at that direct hit. One she probably didn't even realize she'd made. She couldn't know how much he wanted to leave Milano. How badly he wanted to make his own mark.

Feeling his face fold into a scowl, he tilted his head toward the door.

"Ready to call it quits? I'll drive you home."

"What about my car?"

"I don't think you should be driving tonight, do you?" He arched a brow at her empty punch glass.

"I don't feel like I've had that much to drink," she said, peering into the deep glass as if measuring her alcohol levels.

"It'll hit you in about ten minutes," he guessed. Through discussing it, he shifted off the stool and, his hand on her elbow, helped her slide off her seat.

The fur grabbed the fabric of her skirt, though, holding tight so as she slid off, he got a delicious view of her thighs. And those stockings.

Hello, baby.

Tiny roses, tempting lace.

Damn, but she did have a point about how enticing that romance look was.

He was so focused on watching her legs, even though she'd freed her skirt and that beckoning juncture was once again covered, that he forgot to move, throwing her off balance.

"Whoa," she said, falling against him, her hands splayed over his chest as she righted herself. Her curves were sweet and tempting, pressed against his for just a second. Just enough to tease. But not nearly long enough for his tastes.

"I guess you're right," she said, her voice husky. Still a little unsteady, she let go of his chest to push one hand through her hair. "You're going to need to take me."

$$9$$

Pussycats packed a wallop.

Hailey leaned her head against the leather seat of Gage's car and let herself float on the punch-inspired sea of relaxation.

She wasn't drunk.

She'd been drunk a few times. So she should know.

Nope. She was just relaxed.

Her body.

Her worries.

Her gaze shifted from the blur of taillights of the other cars on the freeway to the man driving.

Her inhibitions.

She wished she were drunk. It'd make it easier to do crazy things. The kind of crazy things that wouldn't be smart business decisions. The kind of crazy things that'd make the next week's competition with Gage much, much more difficult.

The kind of crazy things that'd feel oh so incredibly good. Things that followed up on the incredibly good feelings he'd given her earlier.

She'd like an orgasm where she didn't have to be quiet. She'd enjoy having one that included naked body parts. And it'd be even better if most of those naked parts belonged to Gage.

Squirming a little, she dropped her gaze to his lap, and even though it was impossible to enjoy the view since he was seated and driving, she still stared.

Because what she wanted was right there.

Barely aware of what she was doing, she reached her hand out. Maybe to touch it, she wasn't sure.

Before she could, Gage parked the car.

"Why'd you stop?"

"We're here." He tilted his head toward her apartment building. Eyes wide, she followed his gesture. They *were* here. How'd that happen so fast?

He gave her a curious look. "Are you okay?"

She took a quick inventory. Yep, still relaxed. But there was just enough horror coursing through her at the fact that she'd been about to pet his penis to assure her that, nope, she wasn't drunk.

"I'm fine." She offered him a bright smile, then gathered her purse, tucked her scarf tighter into her jacket to battle the chilly San Francisco air and reached for the door handle. "Thank you for the ride."

"I'll walk you up."

"You don't..." *Have to,* she thought, staring at the empty seat and closed door.

Well, then.

She turned to let herself out, but Gage was there, opening her door before she could fumble with the handle. He reached out to assist her from the car. Whether because he was a gentleman, or because he was afraid she'd face-plant it on the sidewalk, she wasn't sure.

"Thank you for the ride," she said, stepping onto the sidewalk with her feet, not her face. Not a hint of swaying, and only the tiniest desire to rub herself against his body. She was doing great.

"I'll see you up."

"It's a secure building." She pointed at the cameras and keypad by the glass entrance. "I'll be fine."

"I'll see you up," he repeated. Then he gave her a cute little shrug. "Hey, it's a guy thing. End of date, see lady to the door."

"This wasn't a date," she murmured. But hey, if he wanted to go inside, ride the elevator up, walk her the thirty feet, then ride the elevator back down, that was up to him.

She just wished he'd keep a little distance between them on the way. He was so close, she could smell his cologne. She could feel his warmth, tempting her to slide closer.

Suddenly nervous, she wet her lips and tried to think of something to say. But nothing came to mind.

Nope. Definitely not drunk.

And not even relaxed anymore.

In silence, she coded them into the building, then punched the button for the elevator. She gazed at the stainless doors as if her blurry reflection was no end to fascinating, trying to pretend she didn't feel the heat of Gage's stare on her face.

Suddenly, all she could think about was the treat he'd served up at dinner. That delicious, mouthwatering orgasm, brought to her by just the tips of his fingers.

It was enough to make a girl beg.

All the more reason to keep her mouth shut. Just in case.

Which she managed to do for the entire elevator ride.

When the doors slid open, she gave him a sidelong glance. Yep, he still looked determined to see her to her apartment. She didn't bother to suggest they say goodbye, and he followed her out of the elevator.

She silently led the way down five doors to her apartment.

"Well, here we are," she said in a cheery tone, pulling

her keys from her purse and giving him an *it's okay, go away now* look. "Thanks for the ride home."

"Thanks for the great double date," he shot back with a grin. Then, probably because he'd got the message from her expression, he leaned one shoulder against her door frame and got comfy.

She rolled her eyes.

"Quit saying that." She put her key in the lock and turned it, but didn't push the door open. "It wasn't a date. And if it was, it was a lousy one, given that half of our double didn't show and the other half spent his time in a room with two women whose ages, added together, still don't equal his."

"Maybe we should try it again, just the two of us," he suggested quietly. So quietly she had a feeling he was just as conflicted by all this crazy passion between them as she was.

The look he gave her was long and considering. Long enough to send the nerves in Hailey's stomach tumbling all over each other. She didn't have to wonder what he was considering. The passion in his eyes said it all.

Her chest hurt with the effort to breathe normally, to not give in to the need to whimper and beg. She stared into those dark, intense eyes, her fingers itching to touch his face. To give him back some of the same delight he'd given her earlier.

She forced herself to be practical. To think straight. In other words, to ignore the pounding desire that was screaming through her system.

"Don't you think that'd be a mistake? You know, since we're competing for this contract and all." She tried to soften her refusal with a smile, wishing like crazy she'd taken her chance with him back when he was still just the guy she'd met at the party.

Or that she was the kind of person who could separate

one thing from the other. Because she wanted him, badly. So badly, it made her ache.

"Yeah. Competitors," he confirmed, his smile falling away. The intensity in his gaze didn't. If anything, it got more powerful. As if he were through searching her mind and was ready to dive into her soul.

"Good night," he said. His words were a whisper over her skin. A soft caress echoed by his hand sweeping over her hair, cupping the back of her head.

She stared, her eyes huge, as he leaned in. Not touching, except his hand to her hair. His lips descended, his gaze never leaving hers. She sighed as he brushed her mouth with the gentle promise of a kiss.

So sweet.

Who knew he had it in him to be so damned sweet. He made her heart melt. And her resolve, dammit.

He shifted the angle, tilting his head to one side and rubbing his lips over her lower one, then taking it between his teeth to gently, oh so gently, tease.

It was as if he'd connected her to an electric wire. Sparks shot through her body, powering up every cell, sending the smoldering passion into flaming heat in an instant. Hailey gasped. Her nipples hardened and wet desire pooled between her thighs. Desire he knew just what to do with, she recalled.

She finally understood what he'd been looking for with those intense stares. The switch that'd turn off her ability to think and turn her body's need to desperate.

It worked, too.

Frantic for more, she shifted the kiss. Her mouth opened, enticing, tempting. Trying to tease him into taking more.

Gage groaned but didn't take the bait. It was as if he was forcing her to make the moves. Daring her to take the role of aggressor.

Okay, then…

Hailey swept her tongue over the seam of his lips, smiling when he opened, letting her in. She sipped, as if he were sweet nectar, until he went wild.

Then he took over.

His tongue plunged, taking hers in a wild, desperate dance.

His fingers tunneled through her hair, holding her captive to his mouth.

Yes.

Excitement pounded through her. On tiptoes, she pressed her body against his, loving that there was no give. Just a brick wall of hard, male flesh.

Releasing her hair, he swept one hand down her back, his fingers curling around the curve of her butt, pulling her closer. Hailey shifted her body so her legs were pressed against his, her core aching, needing more pressure. Needing his touch. His erection, so temptingly hard, pressed against her belly. She wanted to feel it. To see it. Oh, baby, to touch it.

She wrapped one foot behind his calf, then slid it higher, angling herself tighter against his thigh. When her foot skimmed the back of his thigh, he stiffened.

He pulled his mouth away.

Hailey frowned. Forcing her passion-heavy lids open, she gave him a confused look.

"We can't do this."

"Sure we can. If we're lying down, the height difference won't be a problem," she assured him breathlessly, releasing her grip on his shoulder to pat one hand on his cheek.

His lips twitched, but Gage still shook his head.

"We can't. You're drunk."

"No," she told him, giving her head a decisive shake. "I've already done a thorough inventory. I'm relaxed, but I'm not drunk."

"Relaxed?" His eye roll was more a suggestion than an actual move. As if he didn't want to insult her, but couldn't hold back the skepticism.

"I'm not drunk," she repeated. "I can prove it. Come inside. I'll do that sobriety-test thing."

"Why can't you do it here?"

Eyes wide with faux horror, Hailey looked up, then down the hallway.

"Here? Where the neighbors will see and start gossiping? Seriously?"

A silly argument, given that she'd just been wrapped around his body like one of those stripper poles they'd discussed. If the neighbors were the gossiping kind, that would have fueled them plenty. But Gage fell for it, nodding and then slowly—as if he were reluctant to let her go—stepping away.

Hailey turned quickly toward the door to hide her smile.

Dismiss her desire as alcohol-fueled stupidity?

She didn't think so.

This was pure determination. She wanted him, and for the first time in her life, she was grabbing what she wanted and reveling. If that reveling took place naked, so much the better. She wasn't going to worry about how it affected others; she wasn't going to let her fears stop her. She was going to enjoy every delicious second of Gage Milano tonight.

With that in mind, Hailey stepped across the threshold and tossed her purse in the general direction of the hall table. She didn't notice if the clatter meant she'd hit it, knocked everything over, or if her bag was flying across the floor.

She didn't care.

The second Gage crossed the doorway, she slapped the door shut and attacked.

With her body, wrapping it around his as tight and close as she could get with both of them in winter coats.

With her hands, skimming and skating them over his rock-hard form, reveling in the rounded muscles of his biceps under his coat, then across the granite planes of his chest.

With her mouth. Oh, baby, with her mouth. She tasted. She nibbled. She wanted to gobble him up.

For a second, a long enough second to inspire untold neurotic worries in her head, Gage was stone still. Other than the heart beating against her hand, he didn't move.

Shit.

Had she attacked too soon?

Had she misread his signals?

Had that been a pity orgasm over dinner?

Before she could do more than wonder at the depths to which her paranoid mind came up with things to worry about, Gage came to life.

He shoved at her clothes. Her hands pushing his away just as quickly, Hailey shrugged out of her coat and let it fall to the floor at their feet. She wasn't sure who pushed, shoved or pulled, but her scarf and gloves quickly fell, as well.

Their mouths slid, hot and wet, over each other. Tongues tangled in a wild dance, neither leading, both tempting.

He tasted so good.

He felt even better.

Finally, she was able to get her hands on that body. To scope out the hard planes of his chest, to feel the rounded strength of his biceps.

Hailey growled low in her throat, delighting in his shape. In the power of those muscles. He was built. He was hard. He was hers for the taking.

So took, she did.

She nipped at his lower lip, then soothed the flesh with

her tongue. Her fingers made quick work of the knot of his tie, tossing the fabric aside so she could get to his buttons. Then, oh baby, flesh.

She whimpered a little when her hands found bare skin. He felt so good.

She was so focused on his body, on discovering every little delicious bit of it, that she barely noticed how busy he was.

Not until cool air hit the naked skin of her thighs.

He'd unzipped her skirt, so it fell to the floor, billowing over her shoes. His hands skimmed already-familiar terrain, caressing her thighs there, just above the lacy tops of her stockings.

She shivered, even as heat gathered lower in her belly. Her thighs trembled a little, making it hard to balance on her high heels. To compensate, she wrapped one leg around the delicious hardness of Gage's, her heel anchored below his knee. Her core pressed, tight and damp, against his thigh.

"We should…"

"Now," she interrupted. "Here."

Her words were barely a breath, her mind a misty fog. She was pure sensation.

All she could feel was delight.

Sexually charged, edgy, demanding delight.

She wanted more.

She needed more.

Even though she was reluctant to leave the amazing hard warmth of his chest, her quest for more demanded she head south. Her hands slid, fast and furious, down the light trail of hair of his belly, making quick work of his belt.

She wasn't a fashion diva for nothing, so fast did she unsnap, unzip and dispose of his slacks. His boxers went, too, everything hitting the floor with a satisfying thud.

"Babe…"

"No," she protested against his lips, even though she had no idea what he was going to say. She didn't care. This was her fantasy and she was going to lap up every delicious drop.

With that in mind, and grateful for all the fabric on the floor to ease the impact on her knees, she dropped down in front of him.

"Oh my God," he said, his words a low, guttural groan as he stared down at her.

Loving that look on his face, appreciation mixed with fascination, coated with a whole lot of lust, Hailey held his gaze with hers as she leaned forward to blow, gently, on the impressive length of his erection.

Like a lollipop, she ran her tongue from base to top.

Gage's eyes slitted, as though he wanted to close them but couldn't resist watching the show.

The audience adding even more heat to an already-incendiary delight, Hailey shifted higher on her knees so she could wrap her lips around the smooth, velvet head of his penis. Just the tip. She sipped, swirling her tongue in one direction, sucked, then swirled it in another.

Gage's fingers tunneled into her hair, whether for balance or to make sure she didn't stop, she didn't know. She didn't care.

Her mouth wide, she took him in. Slipped her lips down the length of his dick, then back up again. Each time, she tightened her lips, until she was sucking hard, and he was squirming.

Just when his body tensed so much she thought he was going to explode, she pulled back so she was only sipping at the tip again.

"Enough," he growled, swooping down to lift her high, spin her around and pin her against the wall.

His hands raced over her body, slipping down her curves, then back up again. With his lower half pressing deliciously tight against her belly, his erection a tempting reminder of the incredible promise to come, he cupped her breasts in his palms.

Even through the heavy satin of her bra, Hailey could feel the heat as his fingers flexed and squeezed. Needing more, too impatient for him to get there himself, she reached around behind to unsnap her bra, letting the cups fall over his hands.

Gage grunted his thanks, flinging the bra away then grasping her soft, full flesh in his fingers again. His look was intent, laser-focused. As if he was getting as much pleasure from watching the slide of his thumb over her nipple as he was feeling it.

Even if he was, Hailey decided, it wasn't nearly as good as she was feeling. Her head fell back against the wall, her eyes closing so she could focus every single atom of her being on the magic his fingers were working.

He pinched her aching nipple, rolling it around gently, then swiped his thumb over its hardness. Over and over, until she was ready to scream. Heat, tight and wet, pooled between her thighs.

When she squirmed, he shifted. But not, damn him, harder against her aching core. No, he slid down.

His mouth took one nipple in, sucking gently, laving his tongue over and around the aching bud. His hand continued to work the other. Pinching, teasing.

Driving her crazy.

Hailey's fingers slipped through the silk of his hair, holding his head in place as her other hand skimmed over his chest, giving his nipple the same treatment.

He growled.

As soon as he shifted, she did, too, wrapping her leg around him again, this time closer to his waist.

Taking a hint—bless him for being so perceptive—he

released her breast, his hand speeding down her body to cup the hot curls between her thighs.

Welcome back, she thought.

Right at home, his fingers slid along her clitoris in teasing little pinches before plunging into her core.

Hailey exploded.

The power of her orgasm made her whimper at first, then as it built, she cried out, both hands fisted in his hair.

"More," she demanded, greedy and needy.

"Oh, yeah." His words were somewhere between a pant and a growl against her breast.

For just a second, Gage let her go, moved away. Before she could ask, she heard the rip of foil, felt him move away just enough to sheathe himself.

She wanted to help, but by the time she pried her eyes open, he was back in position, his hands on her hips.

Using his support, she lifted one leg up to anchor her foot behind his back. Then the other. There was something wildly erotic about trusting him so much, in believing that he'd keep her from landing on her ass.

His mouth took hers in a voracious, biting kiss.

Hailey's body started the tight spiral toward climax once again with just the touch of his tongue.

He plunged.

She shattered in another miniorgasm.

Her back slammed against the wall at the impact.

Hailey wrapped her legs tighter, no longer worrying that the sharp heel of her stiletto might be cutting into his body.

She needed him to move harder.

Deeper.

And he did.

Plunging.

In and out.

Hard and fast.

Her breath came in gasps.

Her mind swirled in a rainbow of desire, thoughts decimated beneath the power of their passion.

His moves grew jerky. Short. He plunged hard. Paused. Plunged again.

She reached low, gripping the small of his back in her hands, her feet tight against his butt, as she tried to pull him in tighter.

"Baby," he growled, plunging again.

"Do it," she demanded.

As if he'd been waiting for permission, Gage exploded. His jerky thrust sent Hailey spiraling yet again, her body splintering into a million tiny pieces of heaven.

She thought she heard him cry out. She wasn't sure, though, because her mind shut down with the power of her orgasm.

It might have been five minutes, it might have been fifty, before she settled back into her body.

It was still trembling, held against the wall by the hard power of Gage's. Tiny orgasmic quakes still trembled through her.

His breath still came, fast and furious, against her throat.

"Wow," she whispered.

"I think you took advantage of me," he finally said, his words still breathless.

Her head cuddled against his chest now, Hailey smiled.

"Ooh, poor big, tough guy," she teased, her fingers swirling through the hairs on his chest. Finally, she pulled her head back to gaze up at him. "Should I apologize?"

He looked as though he was contemplating that. Then he shook his head.

"Nah. I'll take advantage of you now. Then we'll be even."

Her giggle was cut off to a squeak when he swept her into his arms. Grinning, Hailey wrapped her hands around his neck and crossed her feet at the ankle, loving the view of her stockings and sexy shoes from up here in his arms.

"Bedroom?"

"Down the hall and to the left."

In swift, sure strides, he went that way.

She loved a man who knew how to follow directions.

Now to see what other instructions he might like to follow.

HAILEY WOKE SLOWLY, her body a melting pot of sensations. It was morning, wasn't it? From the patches of light dancing over her closed eyes, it must be. She wanted to stretch, but at the same time didn't want to move because everything felt so good.

But what might feel better was a hot, tasty breakfast of French toast and fruit. A quick mental inventory assured her that she had the ingredients to make Gage a delicious morning-after treat. Then they could come back to bed and enjoy another sort of treat. The naked sort.

And then, riding on a wave of passion and delight, they'd be able to amiably settle this whole silly competition thing. They were two intelligent, clever adults. She was sure they could figure out a way to keep that contract from being an issue. Or, more important, from keeping them off each other's naked bodies.

Finally, more to feed the desperate need to see Gage's face than anything else, she forced her eyes open. A soft, dreamy smile on her lips, she turned her head to the pillow next to her.

Ready to ask him if he liked whipped cream with his French toast, or his other treats, the question froze on her lips.

The pillow was empty.

She shifted to one elbow, looking past the tumbled waterfall of blankets tangled with her clothing from the night before.

His clothes, though, were all gone.

And so was he.

10

THIS FEELING-LIKE-a-complete-prick thing was new to Gage. He sat quietly in the corner of the meeting room, resisting the urge to hunch his shoulders, and tried to shake it off. This was a business meeting.

With a man he'd watched leave the pussycat club in the arms of two women fifty years his junior because he knew sex would hook the guy's vote.

And a woman who refused to look at him. One who was presently pretending he didn't exist, even though she'd blown his mind, among other things, the previous night, who'd provided hour upon hour of the best sex of his life, and whom he'd left without a word that morning. Why? Because he'd got a text from his brother, letting him know their father had called yet another emergency meeting.

So instead of letting Hailey know he was leaving, he'd sneaked out with his shoes in his hands.

Yeah, he was a real prince of a prick, all right.

"As you both know, Cherry's schedule has been somewhat in conflict with this little project. She'd hoped to make it here this morning, but had an unexpected doctor appointment."

"Not that this hasn't been fun," Gage said, shaking off his odd hesitation and leaning forward to give Rudy a direct look. "But how long is this going to drag out? A decision was supposed to be made by today. I don't know about Hailey, but I do know that I have a lot of other things on my schedule that need attention."

Clearly not a fan of being pushed, even when it was to keep his own word, Rudy bristled.

"If you'd like to step out of the game, feel free. That'd make this entire decision much easier."

Gage was tempted.

Dancing to the tune of an eccentric businessman with more power and money than manners was getting old.

And if he stepped off, Hailey would win the contract. Something that obviously meant a lot to her.

But he flashed back to that morning's meeting. Just him, his brother, the old man and the board of directors. All fourteen of them. All wanting to take the New Year in a different direction. None of which Gage gave a damn about, and even more, none of which had required his input. He was marketing. But the old man wanted him there as another token Milano. A show of force. A pawn.

That was another game he'd like to step out of.

And he would. Just as soon as he could do it without giving up his shares in the company or his place at the family table. Although he was willing to negotiate the latter.

"I'm not stepping out," Gage said, reluctantly giving way to the always-present nagging pressure of family obligations. "I'm simply suggesting we finalize this as quickly as possible."

Rudy's glower faded a little and he slowly nodded.

"I agree. But my arrangement with Cherry guarantees her final say in the designs she wears. If I back out, she very well might, too."

Something Rudy looked to be very concerned about. Given that the woman had barely been present so far, he probably had reason to worry.

"As happy as I am to hear that Milano is still in the

competition," Hailey said in a tone that said the complete opposite, "I'd like to make sure you're judging each of the lines fairly. After all, last night wasn't a true test, seeing as you weren't able to experience my presentation."

For the first time since she'd walked in, Gage looked Hailey full in the face. Granted, he was staring in shock at her temerity.

But damn she looked good. Her dress was green, almost as vivid as her eyes. It wrapped around her curves like a lover, sweeping from shoulder to knee with deceptive modesty. He wanted to follow the flow of the fabric, to skim his fingers along the hem, then up under that skirt to touch her soft, warm flesh.

Of course, he'd probably get his hand chopped off if he tried. But that didn't ease the need.

"What you'd have seen if you'd been present at either of our events, Mr. Rudolph, was a sharp contrast between messaging. Romance, which is all about love and happiness, promises not only fabulous sex, but of having it over and over again. That means a variety of lingerie options for each romantic fantasy." She swept her hand through the air, as if waving to a dozen invisible fantasies dancing around their heads.

Gage frowned as Rudy's eyes blurred, obviously taken in by her spiel and focusing on all his own happy fantasies.

"In comparison to the message of sex. Which, let's face it, is impersonal and can be performed just as easily in the nude as in a six-hundred-dollar leather bustier." She gave a tiny shrug, as if saying it wasn't the cost that was a drawback, but the image. "Sex is a physical sensation. Love is an emotion. And while people might be satisfied with sex—they might even crave it—it's the idea of romance and having someone worship them in a physical way that will sell you the most lingerie."

She didn't look Gage's way as she finished, but instead, Hailey gave a sharp nod, all but clapping her hands together. Her smile oozed satisfaction. As it should. Gage was ready to toss aside the leather and go for lace himself.

Then he remembered what was at stake.

"Are you saying romance equals love? You're not really using that as your selling point, are you? Because we, and Rudolph's audience, are savvier than that."

Gage wasn't proud of bashing her argument that way. But dammit, he had to get loose of Milano. He was so sick of playing his father's puppet. He needed that year of freedom, and his chances of getting it were quickly slipping away.

Clearly as impressed with him as he was with himself, Hailey made a show of rolling her eyes.

"I'm saying romance makes people feel good. When they feel that good, they are much more willing to spend money—a lot of money—on keeping the feeling."

She shifted her gaze to Rudy and tilted her head to one side. "Isn't that the point? To not only present a strong visual that will create a trend, but to get people into your store to spend money?"

"Or is it to build an air of exclusivity, something that women will aspire toward and envy?"

Gage didn't go as far as to claim that people—women especially—would pay more for the exclusive designer aura than for the feel-good romantic image.

Because from Hailey's glare, and Rudy's nod, he didn't have to.

"The real question is, which line will better suit Cherry Bella's image and enhance the message Rudolph department stores is trying to send?" Hailey put in quickly.

Rudy heaved a sigh, then watched his fingers tap the desk for a few seconds before he offered them both a grimace.

"Okay, I'm going to be honest with you both. I'm inclined to go with Milano, simply because I think the look is more cutting edge, high-fashion oriented."

Yes! Other than a slight relaxing of his shoulders and tiny twitch of his lips, Gage managed to keep his triumph to himself. But in his mind, he was already packing his bags and heading for Tahoe.

His gaze slid to Hailey, wondering if she might be in the mood for a little snow for the holidays. He frowned. Her face was like porcelain. White, stiff and brittle-looking. Did she hate losing that much? How long would she hold a grudge? Maybe he should send a car for her next week instead.

"But," Rudy continued, drawing out the word in a way that grated up and down Gage's spine. "The decision isn't mine alone."

What? No. He was already on the highway, heading up the mountain. No buts, dammit.

"Of course it's your decision," Gage said quickly, adding a man-to-man smile. "Not that Cherry's input isn't important. But, let's face it, she hasn't been in attendance for much of these meetings. Her priorities are clearly elsewhere."

The old guy pursed his lips. Gage knew that look. It was the screw-everyone, I-want-to-get-my-way-and-be-done-with-this look. He'd seen it on his father's face a million times. Usually right before he waved away every reasonable, well-thought-out and time-intensively researched argument Gage waged.

Kinda like Rudy was about to do to Hailey.

Gage glanced over at her again. Her chin was high, her smile in place. But he could see the hurt and frustration in her eyes.

Crap.

Before Rudy could say anything, and before he could talk himself out of playing hero, Gage gestured to the six-foot mock-up of Cherry surrounded by items from the various lines already chosen.

"But you've put so much time and effort into building a launch around Cherry Bella, you don't want to rock the boat," he said quickly. "She said it herself—the lingerie line is her breaking point. Can't ride roughshod over a woman's choices. You know how that'll come out if you do."

Rudy's grimace made it clear he'd paid the price for doing that a few times in his life. Big surprise.

"Okay, fine," the older man finally said with a huff. "But no more of these clever scenarios. No more romance versus sex. The two of you put together a fashion show, pitch your best spring look. I guarantee, Cherry and I will both attend and the decision will be made within an hour. We need to get on with this."

"When?" Hailey cleared her throat, then started over. "When will we need to do the show? What are the parameters? I mean, how many pieces will you want to see? The designs I pitched were exclusive, intended for your spring debut. I don't have them on hand."

Good point. Gage pulled a face. He was sure that Milano was in the same boat, although he had a hunch Devon had probably already started producing the designs, figuring if Rudolph didn't take them, someone else would.

"I have to get this nailed down," Rudy said, his usually friendly face folding into a scowl. "I can wait a week, maximum. If we can't settle this by then, I'll simply run my spring show without lingerie."

"A week it is," Gage said, his tone quick and hearty. That was six days longer than he wanted, and probably a dozen less than Hailey preferred.

"Fine. The two of you hammer out the details and email

me by the end of the day. I'll green-light it then get hold of Cherry and see you in a week."

With that, a clap of his hands and a nod goodbye, Rudy rose and strode from the room.

Gage waited for the man's size sevens to cross the threshold before turning to offer Hailey a smile.

But purse in hand and black wool coat buttoned, she was already halfway to the door herself.

What the hell?

Wasn't she going to thank him? He'd just given her another chance. Hell, he'd even gift wrapped it.

"Hailey?"

She didn't slow down.

She didn't look back.

And she definitely didn't offer a thank-you.

Seriously?

"Hailey, wait." Gage had to run to catch up with her since she wasn't slowing one bit. How the hell did she move so fast in heels that high?

"Hold up," he said, catching her arm halfway down the hallway. "I thought we'd go out, get something to eat. You know, nail down those details Rudy wants by the end of business."

His charming smile and teasing tone earned him a chilly stare. Damn. He'd known she was one of those women who needed hand holding on the pillow the next morning.

"I've plans for the rest of the afternoon," she said, pulling her arm out of his grasp. "We'll have to settle the details separately."

Awww, she was so cute.

"C'mon," he said, leaning close with his most persuasive smile. "You're just upset that I left when it was three to one in the taking-advantage department and you wanted another shot at me to even it out."

Her eyes went wide, then narrowed in glass-green slivers of fury. Then, in a sweep of those lush lashes, her expression cleared to frosty disinterest.

"You think you were that good?" she asked, giving him an up-and-down look that indicated she was trying to see what he was so proud of.

Burying his irritation, telling himself she deserved to get in a couple of digs since she was hurt, he plastered on his most charming smile.

"Baby, I think *we* were that good."

Her laugh put his charm in the fail column.

"Actually, it has nothing to do with missing out on the various delights you seem to think you are so good at," she said. Her arch look was like a rock, pounding that dagger into his ego just a little deeper. "It has to do with basic manners. If you're a guest at a party, do you walk out or do you take the time to find your host and say thank you for the good time?"

Gage tried to keep his expression smooth, but didn't have much luck holding back the scowl. Was that all she saw it as? A good time? What the hell?

First off, it'd been great. Not good.

And second, she was pissed because he hadn't minded his manners? He wanted to call bullshit on that, figuring it as a face-saving excuse.

But the chilly disdain in her eyes didn't give way to any hint of hurt, no petulant rejection. Nope, just irritated dismissal.

He didn't know how to deal with that.

"I didn't want to wake you. If I did, I wouldn't have been able to resist more." He kept his voice low, but let all the heat he felt ring out, so his words were a little husky. Unable to resist, he risked losing a limb and reached out to trace one finger along the delicate curve of her cheek.

"I knew we'd see each other today at the meeting and figured you'd appreciate some sleep."

Lame. As soon as the words were out he wanted to snatch them back. He didn't need to see her roll her eyes to know that was a suck-ass excuse.

What was it about Hailey that had him so off center? He'd never been this bad at talking to women, had never had any issue charming his way into or out of any situation that involved a female. Then again, he'd never encountered a business deal as weird and difficult to navigate as this one, either.

As the pretty little blonde glaring up at him was the common denominator, he had to figure it was her. Not him.

"Well, thank you so much for considering my needs. And now—" she shifted her arm out of his hold "—I've got an event to prepare for. I'll pull together my notes and email them to you. You can add or adjust as you see fit, then we can send them to Rudy."

In other words, she didn't want anything to do with him.

Pretty freaking insulting, considering she'd jumped his body and sexed him into an orgasmic puddle against her wall.

But if that was the way she wanted to play it?

Fine.

Without another word, not bothering to attempt an argument or another lame excuse, Gage stepped back and let her go.

Just as well. They were business rivals. One way or another, one of them—her, specifically—was going to lose. Better to let it go now, chalk it up to lust and some sexy lingerie and get his life back on track.

Still, Gage had to wonder how many times he was going to watch the sweet sway of her ass as she stormed

away from him. And ponder why he liked the idea of seeing it a few hundred more times.

"HAILEY, HOW'D THE meetings go?"

"Did you wow Rudolph with your vision of romance?"

"Of course she did. Merry Widow designs sell themselves. All our Hailey had to do was show the guy the
lineup, sweet-talk a little and bat those eyelashes, and
boom. We're in for a Christmas treat." To emphasize that,
Jackie did a little happy dance through the warehouse that
sent the jingle bells on her hat, shoes and necklace a din-
gling.

Hailey forced a big smile on her face, sidestepped the
questions and tried to make it to her office. She was way-
laid again to approve a new design change, then a third
time to admire the Christmas tree made of coat hangers
and decorated with bras one of the team had set up in the
corner.

They were all so excited.

Every face in the warehouse glowed, not unheard of
on a Friday afternoon. Or with excitement over the antic-
ipated Rudolph deal.

She'd trained them well.

*Shoot for the stars, and never doubt you'll have a happy
landing.*

What a bunch of crap.

"I've got some samples together for the spring-line
photo shoot on Wednesday," Jackie said, finally through
with her dance. "I know you want to hold off to decide
which pieces we're offering until you know which ones
Rudolph will make exclusive. But I figured it couldn't
hurt to be prepared. I've been shopping for accessories
and props to go with it all."

Jackie gestured to the variety of lingerie, jewelry, shoes
and pretty accoutrements spread across a long, fabric-covered

worktable. "I even picked up some little goodies that I thought would go well with our Christmas pieces, figuring maybe you might want to give Cherry a little gift for the holiday."

Hailey had to blink fast to keep from bursting into tears.

Everyone was so excited. So sure they'd get this account.

Just like she'd been.

Swallowing hard to clear her throat, Hailey tried to figure out when she'd lost her hope.

"That's a great idea," she managed to say, offering a shaky smile. "Thanks for putting in the extra time."

"Oh, believe me, it was my pleasure. This is going to be the best Christmas ever," the younger woman said, all but clapping her hands together. "Don't forget, you have to do the Secret Santa drawing today, too."

"Right." More Christmas cheer. Hailey kept her grin in place as the other woman danced away.

Ho, ho, freaking ho.

As soon as she hit the stairs leading to her office, Hailey let her cheery smile drop, along with her shoulders and her hopes.

"You're late." At the top of the stairs was a loft that spanned the length of the warehouse. Between the top step and Hailey's office was what she often referred to as the dragon-guarded moat. In other words, Doris's desk. Manned, as usual, by the beehive-haired dragon. "You were due here an hour ago."

"You knew I had a meeting," Hailey reminded her in a weary tone.

"You knew it was Friday. I work half days every Friday in December."

Seriously? Knots ripped through her shoulders. On top of everything else, she needed this crap from a woman whose paycheck she signed?

"So leave," Hailey snapped, waving her hand toward the steps and stomping past the huge desk to her own office.

She didn't get any farther than tossing her bag on the chair and her coat on the floor before the dragon stormed in after her.

"You're sure in a grump of a mood. I told you going to all that trouble to try and impress Rudolph was a stupid idea."

Hailey's glower covered Doris, the woman's dour words and the entire day in general.

"I thought you were leaving. Half-day December, remember?"

"I came in to give you your messages," the older woman said with a sniff, her sky-blue-tinted eyelids lowered in a sad puppy-dog look. "Thought they might be important. One from your date last night."

Her heart tumbled, then bounced around her chest in excitement.

"Gage?"

Had he left it before or after the meeting?

Was it an apology for leaving her, naked and wanting, in her own bed?

Or another nagging reminder that they had to figure out their final pitch?

And why did she care so much?

Sure, he'd acted as if he was trying to make nice after his toss-under-the-bus attempt in today's meeting. But she'd trusted him once. She'd got naked with him. And he'd left her.

"I don't want to talk to him," she announced. "If he calls back, tell him we'll handle it by email."

Doris's pout disappeared into a look of speculation. "No. Mr. Rudolph. Isn't that who you were out with? Him and the singer lady?"

Hardly.

But Hailey just shrugged and held out her hand for the messages.

Doris, of course, didn't hand them over. Instead, she kept right on looking as though she was trying to figure out all of Hailey's secrets.

What the hell was it with people inspecting her like this? Her face, her soul, her secrets, they were her business, dammit.

"Another call, too. This one from your mom."

Like a cement block, Hailey's hand dropped to her side. Disappointment settled deep and aching in her belly. She didn't need to hear the message to know what was coming. The same thing as always.

"She said she's sorry. She's not gonna be able to do Christmas with you, after all. Turns out she got a part in a traveling theater troupe and needs to be ready to hit the road on January one."

To her credit, Doris shared the news with a heavy dose of sympathy. Even her wrinkles seemed to empathize, all curving downward with her frown.

"Anything else?" Hailey asked, trying not to feel defeated by a morning determined to kick her ass.

Doris hesitated, then curled the messages into her fist and shook her head.

"Nope. That's it."

How was that for pathetic? The woman who regularly scorned Hailey's rose-colored-glasses-wearing optimism was hiding bad news from her.

"Doris?"

The older woman's sigh whooshed through the room and she gave a jerky shrug.

"Just those Phillips brats, checking to see if you've made arrangements to pay off the business."

Hailey pushed her hand through her hair, wishing she could as easily shove away all the stress tying knots in her scalp. She wasn't ready to throw in the towel, dammit. But, inch by inch, the towel was slipping out of her grasp.

"Maybe it's time to call a meeting," Doris murmured.

Clenching her jaw, Hailey stared at the workroom floor beneath her, clear through the plate-glass window that separated the loft-style office from the rest of the small warehouse.

Below, two desks were manned by her sales team, while her marketing guru was curled up in a beanbag in the corner, laptop in hand. She could see production just beyond the curtains, packaging up the smaller orders that were going out for the holidays.

Her tiny empire, a dozen people total including her and Doris. Wouldn't calling them together for a "we've failed" meeting be tantamount to giving up? Didn't she owe it to them, to herself, to see this through?

"Next week," she said quietly, turning away to meet Doris's oddly patient gaze. "Friday at our monthly meeting. I'll either give them their holiday bonuses or give them as much severance pay as I can pull together."

A week and a half to save her business. Hailey was damned if she'd give up before she had to. Chin high, she held the other woman's gaze, waiting for the slap down.

Instead, after a few long seconds, Doris gave a jerky nod.

"I'll take a look at the books, see what's what. For the bonuses. Or just in case."

Without another word, and with those vile messages still clutched in her talons, Doris clomped out of the room.

Just in case.

Hailey sighed, sinking into her chair and dropping her face to her desk.

Maybe everyone was right.

Maybe it was time she quit believing everything in life would work out if she just held on and had faith.

After all, what'd actually turned out that way for her?

Her father still didn't consider her a part of his *real* family. Her mother blew her off with more ease than a five-year-old making a wish on a dandelion. And now her business, the one thing she'd figured she could count on because she'd built it herself, was imploding.

Tears slid, silent and painful over her cheeks.

And she couldn't do a damned thing about any of it.

11

HER PALM DAMP, Hailey curled her fingers tight. Then with a grimace she shook her hands to air-dry them, curled one again and used it to knock at the heavy oak door.

Okay, maybe *knock* was an exaggeration.

Tap. Lightly.

Still, it counted.

She had to do this. Had to give it one last shot.

She'd wallowed in misery for an entire hour. She'd eaten Doris's entire stash of cookies. And she'd watched her employees, all buoyed up with holiday cheer.

As she'd realized that whether it made her a sucker or not, she had to keep trying. Giving up, it just wasn't her.

Of course, neither were uncomfortable confrontations.

So after another five seconds of silence, she figured she'd given it her best shot and, with a relieved sigh, turned to leave.

"Hailey?"

Crap.

Forcing herself to shift her grimace into a smile—of sorts—she sighed, then turned back around.

"Hi, Gage," she said in that fake, perky-door-to-door-saleswoman tone.

He looked gorgeous. More casually dressed than she'd ever seen him, he wore a plain black T-shirt and jeans with socks. She shifted from foot to foot in her Frye boots, rubbing her gloved finger over the smooth texture of her tights below her black wool miniskirt. Clearly she was overdressed.

As usual, whenever she was around Gage, Hailey had the urge to strip off a few layers of clothes and see what they could do together, naked.

Grateful for the cold night air against her suddenly hot cheeks, Hailey puffed out a breath.

Why was she here again?

Not for that, she reminded herself.

"I was hoping we could talk. Nail down those specifics Rudy wants."

"He wanted them by five." Gage made a show of checking his watch, then gave her an arch look. "That was an hour ago."

"I spoke with him. He's fine with having the information in the morning."

"Ahh, so that's why you've been ignoring my calls and emails." He paused, probably waiting for her to look ashamed. Hailey made sure to keep her smile in place, though. She was tired of other people calling the shots, dammit.

After a second, he shrugged and asked, "Did you send a hooker to his office to persuade him?"

Hailey's lips twitched. Too bad she hadn't thought of that herself. It'd probably have taken less time.

"No. But I did promise that I'd handle everything, including getting Cherry to show up."

"Good luck with that," Gage muttered, stepping away from the doorway to gesture her inside. "Come on in. I'll make coffee."

Hailey hesitated. This was what she'd come for, to talk to him on a casual—hopefully friendly—basis. Which meant going inside.

Still, her stomach did some tumbles as she did.

"Nervous?" he teased, his eyes intent on her face.

"Of what?"

"Good question."

Hailey lifted her chin and gave him a hard look. One she hoped made it clear that she was here for business. Not to see if the sex against his walls was as good as the sex against her walls had been.

Nope. That idea hadn't once entered her head.

Not once.

Because, she assured herself, a few dozen times didn't count as once.

Still, he didn't need to know that. A man who left the morning after without a word didn't deserve any ego strokes. Or to revisit the delights they'd shared.

Dammit.

"Let me take that," he said, gesturing to her purse. She handed it to him, then slipped off her leather gloves to give him those, too.

And, try as she might, she couldn't hide her little shiver as his fingers skimmed her shoulders when he helped her out of her coat.

"C'mon in," he said.

She met his grin with a glower. Yeah. He knew what that shiver had meant.

But once she moved out of the entry and into the living area, desire took a backseat to curiosity.

Wow.

She tried not to gawk.

She hadn't been raised poor by any means.

But Gage?

Clearly he'd been raised rich.

Art, not knickknacks or decorations, but signed-by-famous-people art hung on the walls, was tucked into cubbies, hung from a corner. The furnishings were simple, leather, sleek. But it wasn't cold or, well, fancy.

She noted the pair of tennis shoes kicked off by the couch, the newspaper tossed on the chair.

It was a home.

That shouldn't appeal to her so much.

But it did.

"Is coffee okay? Or would you prefer hot chocolate? Wine? Water?" he offered, playing happy host as he moved through an arched doorway to what, if the hints of stainless she could see were any indication, was surely the kitchen.

She followed, this time not able to hide her appreciative sigh.

"Wow," she murmured. Double oven, a stove and grill, hickory cabinets and granite countertops all screamed kitchen fabulousness.

"Yeah?" He followed her gaze, then shrugged. "I guess. But I mostly order out. Coffee and scrambled eggs are about the extent of my cooking expertise."

"But you offered me hot chocolate." Something she was suddenly craving like crazy, especially if it came with whipped cream.

He lifted a brown-and-white metal tin with a familiar logo. "Heat milk, stir in chocolate."

"No whipped cream?"

His gaze heated, then did a quick skim down her body, as if debating where in particular he'd like to dollop that cream before licking it up.

Hailey's nipples tightened in a silent scream of *here, put it here*.

Focus, she warned herself.

"I wanted to get this entire matter settled, and figured it'd be easier to discuss between just the two of us." She waved her hand between them. "No Rudy, no marketing gimmicks."

No sex.

She managed to keep that last part to herself. Not so much out of concern for saying it aloud. But because she still wasn't completely sure she could—or wanted to—follow that particular mandate.

After a long look, Gage nodded. He moved around the kitchen with ease, gathering a pot, milk, grinding coffee.

Happy to leave the discussion for a bit and just watch him, Hailey settled onto an oak stool cozied up to the work counter. He moved with an economic grace, totally comfortable in the kitchen and with himself.

When he added an extra scoop of chocolate shavings to her hot milk, she tried not to drool. Especially since her mouth wasn't watering over the drink, but the man stirring the spoon.

Maybe this was a stupid idea.

Maybe she should have called instead of seeing him face-to-face. It was much easier to control her urge to lick him over the phone than it was when he was within touching distance.

"So," he asked once they were both settled into the welcoming cushions, their mugs in hand and the fireplace crackling warmly behind them, "are you going to make me an offer I can't refuse?"

"I beg your pardon?" She glanced around the room, an ode to comfortable wealth, then shrugged. What could she offer that he couldn't walk away from?

He leaned closer, the rich scent of roasted coffee and his own cologne wrapping around her like a gentle net, pulling her tight. Making her want to close her eyes and simply breathe him in.

But she couldn't close her eyes, because his were holding her captive. The dark depths promised sensual delights. A promise, she knew from experience, he could meet.

Quite nicely, too.

Hailey's pulse sped up. Her body turned liquid.

Her brain filled with visions of the two of them, their naked bodies sliding together on this couch. On that wall. On any variety of whatever flat surfaces he had in the house.

Would she do him again?

Even though her ego screamed no, for crying out loud the guy didn't even say goodbye in the morning, her body was doing the *yes, please* happy dance.

Her body was much louder, and more enthusiastic than her ego. Her body wanted to touch the hard planes of his chest again. To feel him moving inside her, pounding, throbbing. Sending her spiraling higher and higher.

A little short of breath, Hailey had to pull her gaze away from the hypnotic depths of his.

As soon as she did, logic shouldered its way in, breaking up the fight between ego and desire.

"I don't think I have anything to offer that you'd find irresistible," she stated.

"Wanna bet?" he countered, reaching out to trace his fingers along the curve of her jaw, then down the long line of her throat. The move, so soft and gentle, made her shiver.

He wouldn't be able to refuse sex, between the two of them, in exchange for stepping off the Rudolph account?

"Yeah. Right." She laughed so hard she had to set the mug down for fear of spilling her chocolate. "You'd give up a seven-figure contract for a weekend with my body?"

His eyes were hot on said body, making it difficult for her not to wiggle in place to try to relieve some of the building heat.

"I asked if that's what you were offering."

Nice double speak. For a second, just one, she wanted to say sure. To stand up, strip naked and gesture that he come and get it.

But ego, the part that was afraid he'd laugh if she did, won out. So instead, pretending she wasn't hurt by that image—or by his leaving her—Hailey gave him a sardonic look, then made a show of tapping her fingernail against her lower lip.

"Let's see. Was it only last night that you had full access to my body? Yes, yes, I think it was. And you quite comfortably walked away from it this morning, without so much as a 'see ya, babe.'" She looked him up and down then met his eyes again and arched her brow. "Did something change between now and then?"

Gage set his coffee next to her chocolate before sliding a little closer, so his hard, warm thigh pressed against hers. He ranged his arm along the back of the couch, so close she could almost feel his pulse, but not quite touching her. As if he was crowding all around her, making sure she was very, very aware of his body. But not doing anything about that awareness.

Figured.

Hailey was so sick and tired of people making promises, getting her hooked and emotionally invested, then running out on her. Was there a flashing neon sign over her head, proclaiming her a disappointment junkie?

So instead of giving in to the desire, and the heat Gage was trying to tease her with, she leaned in closer herself.

His eyes flickered, desire flaring before he banked it.

She watched his pulse jump and smiled.

Then, for good measure, she shifted again so her breath wafted over his skin, close enough to leave a haze of chocolate.

"You want to make me an offer, Gage, you go right ahead. But make sure it's one you can keep. I'm tired of being teased."

IT WAS ON the tip of his tongue to offer her anything.
Everything.

In exchange for just one more taste. One more touch. One more wild ride between her thighs.

As if magnetically pulled forward, Gage found himself bending down, his mouth ready to take hers.

And to accept any deal she wanted.

A quick flash of triumph in those green eyes served as a kick-in-the-ass wake-up.

He froze.

What the hell was he doing?

Would he give up his bid for the contract for a weekend with her body?

If the stakes had been only the contract, the answer wouldn't just be yes, it'd be *hell, yes.*

But this was his freedom, a shot at breaking away from Milano, and doing so in a way that didn't destroy his questionable family relationships.

Maybe the better question was, would she give it up for his?

"Why is this so important to you? It's just an account. Albeit a fat one, but it's not like you can't scoop up another dozen fat accounts. You've got a stellar product, a smart sales pitch, and the kudos from being considered for this are enough to parlay into a dozen open doors." Yes, he'd tried this argument once before. But he wanted an answer this time. He'd gone up against some fierce competition in the past, but never one with so much heart, so much determination to win.

Hailey's gaze held his, her eyes more serious than he'd ever seen them. It was as though someone had squeezed all of the bubble out of her personality, leaving her flat. Still sweet, still beautiful, but without the effervescence that was so natural to her.

"I need this contract," she said with a quiet shrug. The kind that said *let it go, just move on.*

But Gage didn't want to.

He wanted to know her. To know what was pushing her so hard. He wanted to know what she had to lose when he won.

"So do I," he countered. Giving in to temptation, he brushed his fingers over the tips of her hair, watching the pale blond strands slide like a silken waterfall back to her shoulder. "What else ya got?"

Her lips twitched, and after a long, considering look, she pulled away and leaned over to get her mug of chocolate again. She didn't sip, just stared into it as if searching for the right words.

"If I don't get this, I'll lose my business."

"How?" Gage frowned. "I did a check on you when I heard we were competitors. You're solid."

"On paper, with the bank, sure." Her shrug was jerkier this time, irritated. "I bought Merry Widow from my mentor three years ago. We had what you'd call a friendly agreement. We both knew the business was worth a lot more if I built it up, kept it going. So we agreed that I'd pay him a set amount each year, and at the end of five years, if I'd doubled the net worth, my debt was paid. Otherwise we'd negotiate fair-market value."

Gage's frown didn't ease, even as he shook his head.

"I don't get it. I mean, it's a crazy agreement, definitely not like anything I've ever heard before. But it hasn't been five years. You're close to doubling your net worth from four years ago so you should be fine." He ignored her look of surprised irritation that he knew so much about her. "So what's the problem?"

"I know it's unorthodox, but it was Eric's way of pushing me. Of motivating me to do my best." She smiled, as if just that memory gave her joy. Then her lips drooped. "Then he died early this fall."

"I'm sorry," Gage murmured.

She nodded, taking a sip of her chocolate. More as a

way to get hold of herself, he figured, than any desire for cooling milk laced with cocoa.

"His kids are calling the loan. Full market value, without credit for previous payments."

"They can't do that."

"Sure they can. Eric and I didn't have a contract. We had a verbal agreement because he didn't want to deal with the drama his kids would put up if they found out what a deal he was offering me."

Pissed now, Gage shook his head. She had to have a good lawyer. Someone who could put an end to the bullshit claim.

"That's crap. I'll get my attorney to look into it," he offered.

For the first time since he'd pushed her on the topic, Hailey's lips curved into a real smile and her eyes danced.

"You are so sweet. But no, it's been looked at. They're within their rights."

"That's crap," he repeated.

"Sure it is. But if I get the Rudolph contract, it'll show a solid enough income that the bank will loan me what I need to pay off the Phillips kids." She sipped the chocolate again, wrinkled her nose and returned the mug to the table. "So there you go. My reason for needing the contract."

It was pure crap. Gage didn't bother to say it a third time, though. Instead, he silently fumed. Not because her needs put him in a difficult position, although they did.

But because she'd been screwed over, royally. Because some lame ass was too worried about upsetting his kids, Hailey was in danger of either losing her business or going deep into debt. A debt that, if he'd written up the agreement as promised, she'd never have had to take on.

Damn.

Suddenly, all he wanted was to make her smile. To show her how important, how special, she was.

He didn't have words, though. And even if he did, he'd feel like a complete idiot spouting off that kind of thing.

So he offered what he had.

A soft, sweet kiss.

A promise.

To worship her.

To take care of her.

To make sure her needs, her satisfaction, were primary.

Hailey's eyes were huge as bright green saucers as she pulled her mouth away from his.

"What's that for?"

"Because you deserve to feel good about yourself."

She gave a little laugh, as though she thought he was kidding.

Then, seeing that he was 100 percent serious, her smile faded. Desire, hope and something deeper washed over her face.

"You think so?" she asked, hesitating before running her fingers, just the tips of them, along his jaw.

Gage leaned into her hand, loving the feel of her.

"Spend the weekend with me."

Her gasp was sharp. Her pulse jumped in her throat. And those glorious eyes of hers filled with questions. He didn't know the answer to most of them, though. So he lifted her hand in his and brushed a kiss along her knuckles.

"Spend the weekend with me. Let me show you how special I think you are."

She pressed her lips together, then sighed and gave him a tentative smile.

"And how were you planning to do that?"

"Like this," he promised, grabbing the invitation and opportunity fast, before she changed her mind.

Just like he took her mouth.

Fast.

Hard.

Intense.

With every bit of passion and need and desire he had for her.

Her body melted into his as he pulled her onto his lap. Her lips gave way to his tongue, welcoming him into her warmth.

And suddenly, the only thing Gage wasn't sure of was if a weekend was enough time to show her how amazing she was.

12

"THIS IS RIDICULOUS. I can't believe I let you talk me into it."
Gage huffed, giving the woman responsible a hard look.
Difficult, since she was so adorable wrapped only in one
of his dress shirts and a layer of body lotion.

Lotion he'd slicked on himself after their shower that
morning.

The memory of that soft, smooth skin under his hands,
of the slide of the thick lubricant beneath his fingers,
stirred an interest in Gage's body. One that had nothing
to do with the crazy ideas Hailey was trying to get him
hooked into.

"C'mon. It'll be fun. I can't believe you've never done
this before."

"It's not like we're talking exotic sexual positions or
kinky toys, Hailey." He hunched his shoulders, really wishing they were. In those, he had experience in spades.

"No. As fun, exciting and important as those all are—"
she paused to give him an eye roll and a teasing smile
"—this is all of that, too."

Gage sighed.

Then, showing every bit of the reluctance he felt, he
approached the corner of the room with trepidation and,
giving her a grumpy look, took the thread she'd filled with
popcorn and tried to figure out what to do with it.

"I'm supposed to, what? Throw this over the branches?"

Hailey gave him a look that said she couldn't quite believe his professed cluelessness.

"Here, do it like this," she said, showing him how to drape the popcorn-covered string.

He really should be worried, because he was starting to think she could talk him into anything.

He'd figured the fact that he had no tree was a good enough excuse when she'd asked why he hadn't decorated. But no. She'd hauled on a pair of his sweatpants, pulled on her boots and swaddled herself in one of his sweaters before hauling him down to the corner lot to choose a tree.

He'd been so entertained by the seriousness with which she studied each specimen, rounding every tree and staring at it as if coded somewhere inside was the key to Santa's nice list. Finally, when he'd tried to grope her behind the wreath display, she'd settled on a tall, skinny one, claiming it'd be easiest for them to carry back.

Carry. He'd trotted down the San Francisco streets with a woman wearing his sweats and five-hundred-dollar boots, carting a pine tree.

What else could he do once they got it inside but strip her naked and make love to her?

Now, three hours and a handful of orgasms later, she was standing there, arms akimbo, giving him the hurry-up look.

"Isn't it enough to have the tree? Why does it need crap hung from it?"

"Because it's Christmas. Hanging crap from a tree is part of the holiday fun." She finished wrapping the string of lights they'd bought along with the tree, then bent low to plug it in.

Gage tilted his head sideways, grinning. He had to admit, the decorating view was definitely fun.

"Haven't you ever had a tree before? Ever?" she asked, pausing from her study of the perfect placement of lights

to give him a puzzled look. "Does your family not celebrate Christmas?"

"Sure, we celebrate. But the tree always just sort of
showed up in the lounge—lights, balls and presents."

Depending on which stepmother was ruling the roost at
the time, it might be glinting with crystals or wrapped in
yarn. One year, it'd had tiny porcelain dolls hanging from
the boughs. That'd seriously freaked him out.

"I guess that's part of your fancy upbringing, huh?"
she teased.

"I never thought it was fancy," he said honestly, trying to hang the popcorn strands the way she had, so they
draped instead of tangled to look like something a bird
puked up. "I mean, the house was huge and there might be
a lot of social stuff going on, depending on the stepmom
du jour. My brother and I were in boarding school most
of the year, so when we'd come home for winter break,
the tree was there. Done. If we ever decorated when I was
little, I don't remember it."

Hailey paused in her adjusting and tweaking of the
lights to glance at him, those big eyes of hers filled with
tears.

"You were sent away."

"More like allowed to run away," he said with a laugh.
"Don't feel sorry for me. I loved boarding school. Anything was better than the revolving circus that was that
house's inhabitants."

She straightened, moving closer and giving him a look
so deep with compassion that Gage actually felt his heart
melt a little.

"Were you hurt there?"

His freak-out over the deep emotions she was inspir-
ing gave way to shock. "What? Hurt? Nah. It was just
crazy. My old man was a womanizer. Think Rudy, with
less money and more to prove. We used to joke that he

should lease wives instead of marrying them, since he traded them in as often as his cars."

"And that didn't bother you?"

"Why? None of them stuck around long enough to matter, so it wasn't like I missed them when they were gone."

It was only after a few seconds of silence, and his irritation with the strings of popcorn tangling together, that Gage glanced over.

Mouth open, eyes wide with sympathy, Hailey was staring at him as though she wanted to wrap him in her arms, pull his head to her shoulder and hug away all his hurts.

He figured he didn't have any, but he'd be willing to let her try, anyway.

"Don't make it into a big deal. It really isn't," he said honestly.

"What about your mom? Were you really young when she left?"

"Four and a half," he said with a shrug. "She came around a few times, I think, before she was killed in a car accident. But it's not like I grew up thinking there was a big hole in my life. It's just what it was, you know? One way or another, it was my dad, my brother and me. And a predecorated Christmas tree."

She didn't laugh.

"I'm done with the threaded popcorn," he said, tossing on the last bit in hopes of changing the subject. "Are we done or do you want more crap on the tree?"

"More crap," she said absently, handing him a stack of intricate snowflake shapes—cut from paper stolen from his office—that she'd cut out and hung on the same string she'd used for the popcorn.

"You must be really close to your brother, then."

So much for a subject change.

"At the moment, I'm almost tied. But by next year, I'll be ahead," he murmured absently.

Damned right he would. Devon had used his two-year advantage most of their life to stay in the lead, but a year off with no Milano emergency demands, and Gage was sure he was gonna sprint into first place.

"What?" Hailey shook her head. "What do you mean? Ahead?"

"You know, ahead. As in, which one of us is winning. Devon and I compete. Best grades, higher SATs, board support, bigger piece of the wishbone." He grinned, re-membering. "That Grinch costume? I lost the wishbone bet at Thanksgiving and that's the price I paid. That's the kind of thing we do."

She squinted, as if trying to see through his words to the truth beneath. Why? He didn't understand her confusion.

"You're trying to tell me that the entire basis for your relationship with your brother is competition?"

Gage frowned. She made it sound so unhealthy.

"Sure."

"C'mon. No fraternal bond? No shared interests? Not even sibling rivalry?" She shook her head as if that were impossible to believe.

"Isn't sibling rivalry basically the same thing as com-petition?" After she gave a slow, considering nod, he shrugged and said, "Sure, we've got that. And we've got plenty of mutual interests. I check out his investments, ad-vise him on marketing. He checks out mine, advises me on expansion options."

"That's it?" she asked.

He didn't know why she looked so horrified. Since it made him feel a little defensive, he racked his brain try-ing to find other examples for her.

"We aren't friends, like the kind who hang out together, but we respect each other. Family loyalty goes a long way, too. Shared life experiences, heritage, that kind of thing. But the bottom line is, we both want success. We both want to be a part of the family business, but we want it on our own, too. We both want to win."

He could see she wasn't buying his assurance that he wasn't emotionally scarred or harboring some hidden resentment of family-centered holidays. Rather than trying to convince her that, yes, he really was that shallow, he turned the tables.

"What about you? Now, granted, I was mostly focused on other things at your apartment the other night. Like your naked body and how incredible you felt under my fingers." He waited, then gave a satisfied smile when she blushed. "But I didn't see that you had a tree up."

Her expression changed, the frown seeming to turn inward before she slipped on a smile.

"I was waiting for my mom. It used to be our special tradition, and since she was visiting this holiday, I wanted to do it together. When I was little, we always decorated together as a family the weekend after Thanksgiving. After my parents divorced, I spent Thanksgiving with my father, so my mom waited until I was home and we did the tree together."

He tried to imagine her as a little girl, those flaxen curls in pigtails and some cute footsie pajamas on while she hung candy canes from the low-hanging boughs. He'd bet she'd been adorable.

"So you got to do two trees? No wonder you love this kind of thing."

"No. Just the one tree. My dad married the same year as the divorce, and Gina, my stepmom, liked to wait until closer to the holiday."

Leave it to the stepmom to shove the kid out. Gage had seen enough of it growing up to recognize the signs. He didn't even need Hailey's stiff upper lip, lifted chin or downcast eyes. And while he'd learned by seven to shrug it off, she was still carrying it around.

Time to quit bitching about the decorations, he decided. If a tree made her happy, they'd decorate. Hell, he'd take her to his father's place and she could decorate there, too.

"When's your mom arriving so you can do your tree?" I.e., how long was she available for freewheeling, wild and constant sex before family nabbed a portion of her attention?

On tiptoes, trying to wrap a thread around a high branch, Hailey went board stiff, dropping back to the flats of her feet. The snowflake was still in her hand, though. Its ripping sound was like fingernails on a chalkboard. Loud, invasive and painful. She grimaced, then crumpled the ruined decoration in her fist before shrugging.

"No mom this year. She called Friday and left a message. Something came up and she can't make it."

Did everyone let her down?

Underneath the hurt in her eyes, Gage could see acceptance. As though this kind of thing happened all the time.

"Well, hey, we'll go decorate your tree after this, okay? Just you and me. I'll bet you have actual decorations and stuff, right? So we can eat the popcorn instead of tossing it on the branches?"

As soon as the words were out, he realized he'd just volunteered to step in and play family. That was a serious thing. A way past *let's get naked and slide all over each other* thing. For a second, he wanted to grab the words back. Or change the subject. Then, as he watched her face melt into a beautiful smile, he realized he kinda liked it. Liked her trusting him. Believing in him.

"So what do you think?" he asked, gesturing to the tree. "Am I assistant material?"

"You're a great assistant." Her words were a little husky and her smile a little shaky, but—thank God—she didn't do anything crazy, like cry.

Whether because she wasn't a teary kind of gal, or because she could see how uncomfortable he was, she put on a bright face instead and looked at the tree.

"It still needs something," she decided, tilting her head to the side, as if she were critiquing an outfit about to hit the runway. Gage figured it must be a girl thing, since the tree looked fine to him. "Do you have anything shiny? Old jewelry, CDs, anything foil?"

Seriously?

He gave her a look, then glanced at the tree, then back at her. She had that stubborn tilt to her chin again, and her eyes were all soft and sweet.

Dammit.

"Let me see what I can find."

THAT WAS ABOUT the weirdest tree she'd ever seen. And given that there was one in her warehouse right now made of coat hangers and bras, that was saying something.

Gage's arms loose around her waist, Hailey leaned back against his chest and sighed.

"It's perfect," she decided.

"Okay."

"It is." Laughing, she turned in his arms, cupping her hands behind his neck and giving him a quick, smacking kiss. "You done good."

He cast a doubtful eye over her shoulder, clearly seeing the actual tree and not the sentiment hanging from its boughs.

"Okay," he said again.

Then, as if there was nothing else to say about a tree covered in foil condom wrappers, popcorn and paper snowflakes, he laughed, shook his head, then took her mouth.

Hailey let the power of his kiss take her over, pull her down, permeate her being.

Being with Gage was like being wrapped in warmth.

Not just the fiery heat of passion, although that was a constant and definitely keeping her excited.

But the laughter. The kisses. The gentle teasing and constant interest in her.

Her views. Her ideas. Her past and her present. What she wanted in the future, even. She'd never had anyone so focused on her. Just…her.

As though he really cared about her.

Breathing in deep, she pushed away the sudden tears that thought brought and focused on the kiss.

Her lips danced over his, her hands sliding gently, oh so gently, over his naked skin. Satin over steel.

They fell into the lovemaking with a gentle sigh.

Every move was a whisper. A breath of skin against skin. A tease of a kiss, a wash of warm air, wrapping them together in a sweet, dreamy sort of passion.

As Gage's body ranged over hers, Hailey stared up into the endless depths of his eyes and opened herself, welcoming him in.

As he moved, slowly sliding in and out, she held his gaze. She let everything she felt shine in her own.

The delight.

The desire.

The deep, intense emotions that she couldn't even put a name to herself.

He never looked away.

Even as she tightened, as passion caught her in its needy web, her body demanding total focus, complete attention, he still watched.

And when she went over, the desire pounding and swirling through her in deliciously hypnotic waves, he smiled.

A slow, satisfied smile.

And then with a low moan, he joined her.

Two hours later, wrapped together in front of the fire,

Hailey was still trying to come to grips with the power of their lovemaking.

Her eyes fixed on the flickering flames, the lights of the Christmas tree a soft glow against the wall, she tried to identify the feelings inside her.

Peace. Joy. Love.

Scary.

"Look," Gage finally said, shifting onto his elbow. "Next year, I'll have a lot going on. I'm going to be really pushing to get my own business solid fast. It's going to take focus and time."

Hailey froze, body and heart.

Well, at least he was being honest, she told herself, wrapping the sheet closer, trying to stave off the shivers. Still, she'd never been blown off while naked before.

"I'm going to take care of this whole thing with Rudolph, with saving your company. I don't want you to worry about it anymore," he said, his words quiet, measured. Her heart thumped a few extra beats before Hailey could catch her breath and turn in Gage's arms to face him. "I'll fix everything, okay?"

For a brief second, Hailey wanted to protest. She didn't need favors. She could win the contract on her own, without him stepping aside for her. But Rudy had already made it clear that if it were only up to him, he'd go with Milano. And she couldn't afford to put all her faith in Cherry, or to let pride stand in the way of saving her business.

"Are you sure?"

"Yeah. Totally sure."

"And the presentation on Tuesday? Should we cancel?"

His frown flashed for a second. "Nah, it's more professional to keep it. I'm sure I'll have everything taken care of, but it's a good fallback just in case, too."

Just in case.

Her heart melted, the entire world taking on a rosy glow.

He really was taking care of her.

"And us?" she asked, feeling as if it were Christmas morning and Santa had not only brought her entire list, but had doubled up on the things she hadn't even thought to ask for.

"After this deal with Rudolph is done, I want to make us a priority," he said, brushing the hair off her cheek and giving her a tender look. "It's going to be hard, but I want to make sure we get time together. It might take some juggling, maybe a few cancellations or rescheduled dates here and there. Are you okay with that?"

Hailey blinked.

"What?"

"I want us to be together. I want to build on this, to see where we go," he said, gesturing between their bodies before sliding his hand into her hair to caress the back of her head. "I want to give us a chance."

A chance.

He wanted her. Them.

Without any prodding or girlie manipulation, he'd straight-up claimed them a couple.

Hailey's smile started slow, tremulous, since she refused to cry. But then the giggles took over and she pressed her free hand to his cheek, pulling his face close for a kiss.

Then another.

And yet another, this one turning hot.

Sweet passion poured over them. She shifted, pressing his body down against the floor, the warmth of the fire flickering over their entwined forms.

Gentle kisses, soft caresses gave way to heat.

Grateful for his resourcefulness, she stretched over, tugging one of the glinting foil condom packages from the tree. She quickly sheathed him, then before he could do more than moan, she slid onto the hard length of his erection.

Together, with her taking the lead, they made slow,

sweet love again. This time, he came first. The feeling of him, throbbing and pulsing inside her, sent Hailey over, too. She collapsed, breathless, onto his chest and gave a purr of satisfaction.

"I take it that's a yes?" he murmured against her hair as they were shivering with orgasmic aftershocks.

He didn't elaborate. He didn't have to. She knew he was asking if she wanted to give them a chance.

Hailey's laugh was a whisper, nuzzled close against his throat.

"Yes. Definitely yes," she agreed.

With just the flickering warmth of the fire, and Gage's body, covering hers, Hailey drifted off to sleep. Her last thought before sliding under was to wonder if she should be happy that the contract was hers. Or terrified that she'd had to fall in love to get it.

HAILEY WAS ALMOST skipping as she made her way up the steps of the Rudolph building.

This was it. The last presentation.

She and Gage had told Rudy Friday night, before their delicious weekend together, that they'd meet on Tuesday for one final time.

Each would bring the designs they felt most represented the line, a marketing plan they planned to implement to support the Rudolph debut, and their final pitch. Even though it wasn't going to be necessary, since Gage was backing out of the contract, Hailey had still prepared as if this was the most important day of her life. And, she thought, bubbling over with optimism, it just might be.

As she exited the elevator and headed for the boardroom where they were to meet, Gage came hurrying toward her. She melted a little at the sight of him and that gorgeous smile.

"Hey, you," she said, brushing her fingers over his

cheek as if it'd been weeks since they'd been together instead of that morning. "I missed you."

"Ditto," he said with a grin. Then he tilted his head toward the double doors at the end of the hall. "I tried to reach you. Didn't you get my message?"

"No, what's up?"

"I came in early, met with Rudy." Tucking his hand under her elbow, Gage led her toward the boardroom doors as he spoke. "We're good to go. So I borrowed his boardroom to show you the setup."

Setup? He'd set things up for her?

Hailey all but clapped her hands together, she was so excited.

Together, they stepped into the boardroom. There, to one side by a set of open doors, were the samples she'd sent ahead for her presentation.

On the opposite end was a huge whiteboard. On it was a list of company names, some she recognized as huge. A marketing schematic covered one half of the board. She squinted. The schematic had her name at the top.

Trepidation started to overtake excitement in her stomach.

"What is this?"

"Rudy's going with Milano for the spring account, of course. He wanted to all along, but knew Cherry was leaning toward Merry Widow. But she's been so out of the loop, he's decided not to depend on her input any longer."

He said that as though he hadn't sold her out. As if just because Rudy would have chosen him in a head-on battle, that meant it was okay that he hadn't stepped down like he'd promised.

"You're kidding, right?"

"Nope. No joke. I got this all put together for you. You've got guaranteed orders, double the clientele as I'd suggested earlier and enough interest in your lingerie to translate into a fat load of new business." He pointed to the two-dozen names he'd listed on the board. Next to each was a dollar figure. Not shabby figures, either.

Hailey's head was buzzing.

"I put together a marketing plan for you. Now, granted, this is a first draft since we haven't talked it through and I don't have your actual figures or your business plan to integrate into it. But with it, and the prospectus I created, you have enough to take to the bank and get a big enough loan to stave off those greedy assholes."

His smile was huge, his eyes dancing. He looked as if he'd just handed her a pony covered in glitter with rainbow ribbons tied to its mane.

Instead of killing her dreams and stomping all over them.

"I can't believe you did this." Her head spinning, she shook it and hoped everything would shift. Change. Turn out to be a big fat hot-chocolate-induced mirage.

But it didn't.

Nope. Still there, on the board in bright colors, was proof that Gage had screwed her over.

And there he stood, grinning and looking as if he expected a thank-you note.

13

HAILEY WAS PACING the boardroom, from one end piled high with lingerie samples to the other with its whiteboard and presentation details.

As gorgeous as she was, with her skirt swishing to show a tempting length of thigh with each turn, he didn't think she was happy.

"What's up?" he asked, grabbing one of the leather chairs and pulling it out from the table so he could sit.

Then he caught the look on her face.

Pure fury, wrapped in a layer of hurt.

Nope. He was better standing.

"You stabbed me in the back." The accusation was made through clenched teeth.

"What the hell?" He reared back, shocked at both the accusation and the fact that his sweet Hailey could pull together this much anger.

"I thought you said you were going to let me have the contract."

"I said I was going to make sure you were taken care of," Gage countered. "I offered this before, and now it's an even better deal. I've got a dozen stores, venues and even a TV show all lined up, each one ready to make huge purchases. The revenue in a year will be as much, if not even more, than the Rudolph deal."

He waited, sure she'd simmer down now.

But she didn't. If anything, the fury in her eyes got even more fierce.

Gage frowned, starting to worry a little. He hadn't misplayed this. He was sure of it. There was no question that he was going to have everything he wanted. It looked as though it was just going to take a few pats and soothes before he got there.

"Hey, you haven't heard the bonus yet. By getting the Rudolph contract, I get my freedom. I can take on any client I want. So not only are you getting a boatload of new clientele, you get me." His smile was pure triumph, and he held out his arms, ready for her to throw herself at him in gratitude.

She hissed. If she'd been a cat, he was pretty sure she'd be wearing his skin under her nails right now.

He dropped his arms.

"I don't get it," he said. "You want success, or do you want the Rudolph deal? Aren't you being a little shortsighted with this obsession of yours?"

"We had an agreement."

Gage nodded.

"Right. We agreed that I'd make sure you were taken care of, that you didn't lose your business."

"That's not what I agreed to."

He sighed, shoved his hand through his hair, trying to figure out where this had all gone wrong.

"I can't help what you thought," he said. "I never said I'd step off the campaign. I made it really clear why not."

"And I made it really clear what this meant to me, and why I had to get the account."

He'd be able to handle this a lot better if she didn't sound as if she was about to cry. Gage hated feeling like a jerk. Hated even more the sense that his perfect solution was turning all to hell right before his eyes.

Dammit, he wanted Hailey.

And he wanted his freedom.

She just had to get over this silly attachment to the Rudolph account, and he could have both.

HAILEY SHOVED BOTH hands through her hair, hoping that if she tugged hard enough, a solution would pop out of her head.

When she'd woken up that morning, her world had been perfect. She'd been sure her business was safe, her holidays were heading toward the most awesome of her life, and she was falling in love with the greatest guy in the world.

Hailey had a brief, pining wish to return to that moment. Whether to rejoice in its brief existence, or to slap herself for being so naive, she wasn't sure.

But the moment, and the hope, was gone.

And this was her damned reality.

"Why would you do this?"

"You always take care of everyone else. You're the fix-it girl. The sweetheart who sweeps in and makes everyone feel better. Your employees, your family. Hell, even me. But who makes *you* feel better?" Gage's grin was part triumph, part little-boy-at-Christmas excitement. "I want you to have everything, too. So I fixed it so you could."

"No, you fixed it for you," she said quietly.

"Babe, this way we both win. You get to keep your business. I get my freedom. We both get to be together. That's better than a win-win. It's a win-win-you-and-me-win."

He looked so happy, so pleased with himself.

A part of her, the part that wanted everyone happy, wanted to step forward and give him a big hug. To give him the praise and gratitude he clearly expected. But as Hailey chewed her lower lip until it felt raw, she couldn't force out the applause he expected.

It wasn't as though she wasn't used to betrayal.

It wasn't as if this was the first time someone had made her a promise, then blithely danced away from it.

But this time, it was too much.

This time, she couldn't smile and pretend she was okay with it.

Pretend she didn't mind always coming in second. Because when it came to a commitment between two people, coming in second meant coming in last.

"C'mon, Hailey, let's just move past this," Gage said, his smile pure charm.

"We can't just move past it. I can't." She shook her head. "You're like everyone else. Happy enough to say you're there for me, as long as it's convenient."

"That's not true."

In other words, he didn't want it to be true.

Hailey looked at her shoes, ready to give in. She caught a glimpse of the lingerie samples out of the corner of her eye. She was losing it. Without that contract, there was no guarantee she could keep her business. And she was about to brush that off because it might make Gage feel bad?

So she took a deep breath and met his eyes. And even though each word was painful, she forced herself to speak.

"I've spent my entire life afraid that if I ever spoke up, ever put myself and my needs ahead of my parents' self-interest, that I'd be rejected. That they'd prove, beyond just the whispers in the back of my mind, that they couldn't—that they wouldn't—set aside their own self-absorbed priorities for me."

His frown was ferocious. Whether the anger was directed at her, or at himself, didn't matter. Hailey didn't care. For the first time in her entire life, she only cared about her feelings. It was both liberating and absolutely terrifying.

"You're putting other people's crap between us here,"

he accused. "You have a good reason to have those issues. But I shouldn't need to pay for them."

"But you're doing the same thing." How could he not see it?

Gage shook his head, as if denying her words could deny the truth.

"You're saying you won't take this deal?" he asked, as if he needed to hear her spell it out in tiny letters before he'd believe it.

"I'm saying I will not take your consolation-prize accounts. They're not enough to save my business. They're not enough to pay off the Phillips kids and put an end to this drama," Hailey repeated. Then, even though it was hard to get the air past the knot of tears in her throat, she added, "And if you can't understand why, we can't be together."

In that very second, she felt so miserably selfish.

It wasn't exactly an encouraging feeling to do this kind of put-herself-first crap again, she had to admit.

"You're not thinking straight. C'mon, seriously? You'd throw us, and a golden array of contracts, over? For what? Ego?"

Nope. Not encouraging at all.

But thankfully, anger stepped in and kept the apology on Hailey's lips from spilling out.

"Ego? How is my refusing to take second—no, last place and make the best of it ego driven?"

"You just said it yourself. You have to win, so you have to have first place."

"Me?" Hailey thumped herself in the chest so hard, she almost fell over. "Are you kidding? You're the one who won't walk away from this because you're afraid to go it alone."

"Don't be ridiculous," he dismissed. He looked derisive, but his hunched shoulders and scowl told her she'd scored a direct hit. "It's not as simple as leaving a lucrative job for a start-up. If I walk out, I'm giving up my heritage. I'm giving up any future claims on a company that's been in the family for a half century."

Maybe it was because she'd never had that kind of familial obligation—and definitely never had anyone in her family feel obligated to her—but Hailey couldn't wrap her mind around it.

"You're doing a job you don't like, at the beck and call of people you say don't respect you, because…what? You're afraid you won't get your share of the pie somewhere down the road?"

"Don't try to make it sound so stupid."

"I didn't have to try."

Gage ground his teeth, probably to hold back the cussing, but couldn't keep still. He paced. He grumbled. He did everything but look at Hailey.

"I just tried to hand you the best of everything, and you're tossing it aside. You have a bad habit of that, I've noticed."

Nice way to turn it around on her. But Hailey wasn't playing that game.

"Oh, please. I've never had anything handed to me," she snapped.

"No? What about Merry Widow?"

Before she could tell him how stupid and off base that was, he continued, stepping closer, butting right into her personal space to look down into her face.

"Your old mentor gave you the business. Yes, you had to work hard. You had to make payments. But if it wasn't for him, you wouldn't have had it."

"That's not the same. He and I had an agreement. One that if he were alive would mean I could walk out this door and not have to deal with you, this stupid contract or jumping through any of these ridiculous hoops." Hailey dropped back onto her heels, a little surprised—and a tiny bit ashamed—to realize that last had been offered at a full-on scream, from tiptoes so she could better get in his face.

Hmm. Maybe she had a few issues to resolve.

"Right. You had an understanding. You with obligations on your end. Him with obligations on his end. He didn't meet his, did he?"

"He met his obligations," she retorted, biting off the words. Eric would never have deliberately hurt her.

"Why didn't he draw up a contract for the purchase of the business, then? Why do you, all of a sudden, have to fork over the remaining balance if you had an agreement?"

"Because his kids—"

"If you had a contract, they couldn't do a damned thing."

Hailey pressed her lips together, trying not to burst into tears.

She'd trusted Eric. Just like she'd believed her father when he said she was always his little girl and had faith in her mother's vow to keep their family together.

But Eric, her mentor, her friend, her confidant, hadn't wanted to put it in writing because it'd upset his kids if they found it. And he didn't want to deal with their drama, as he put it.

Hailey should have insisted.

She should have pushed.

But she'd been so grateful to have the business, so grateful to be making her dream a reality, that she hadn't wanted to rock the boat. As always, she hadn't wanted to ruin a good thing by appearing greedy.

By trying to take care of herself.

When would she learn that nobody, ever, put her needs over their wants?

"Will you please leave?" she asked, near tears.

"No. We need to settle this."

"I don't want to discuss it. I don't want to talk to you." She clenched her jaw to keep her lips from trembling, but couldn't keep the tears from filling her eyes.

"Hailey—"

"Just go. I can say my goodbyes to Rudy without you. You've done enough. You can't give up this account— even though you admit my designs are better—because you won't get your perfect outcome wrapped in a perfect ribbon and your daddy won't love you anymore. Fine."

Before he could respond, before she rushed to apologize for the unfairness of her words, she waved him away.

"Please. Go."

"We haven't settled this." Gage's hand was warm on her shoulder as he tried to turn her to face him, but she shrugged it off. "There's more between us than just some silly business issue. Don't throw this away, Hailey."

She took a deep breath, then another to try to control her sobs. She'd never felt so good as she did with him. So wanted. But she couldn't be with him. Not now. It took all her strength, but she forced herself to turn and face Gage.

"We're through. Whatever we might have had, or could have been, it's over now." She gave a tiny, helpless sort of shrug. "Call it a quirk of mine. I don't want anything to do with the person responsible for pounding that final nail in my business's coffin."

Unable to resist, she indulged herself one last time by reaching out to cup her hand against his cheek. His eyes full of anger and pain, Gage leaned into her fingers, turning just a little to nuzzle a kiss against her palm.

It was too much. Hailey had to go.

Without looking at him again, she pulled her hand away, skirted around him and ran through the open door at the far end of the boardroom so fast, she was surprised she didn't fall and break her neck.

She'd leave. Oh, God, she wanted to leave. But she had

to be a good businesswoman. Smart women didn't burn bridges. She had to say her goodbyes, leave on a good impression.

But she couldn't until she got hold of herself.

Telling herself to get a grip, the sooner she stopped freaking out, the sooner she could get the hell out of here and go home, she hurried through the small anteroom she'd left her lingerie samples and supplies in. She shut the door behind her, blocking off Gage and the boardroom.

And almost screamed, her boots skidding across the carpet as she tried to stop her forward momentum.

"Cherry?" Hailey winced. She'd had no idea the other woman was even there. After how many attempts to get the torch singer to show up and listen to one of her brilliant pitches, and she finally did. And what did Hailey do? Have a total emotional breakdown, throw over her lover and kiss her career goodbye. All in one screaming match.

Lovely.

"You're smart to let him go," the other woman said, her voice huskier than usual.

Hailey was about to agree when she looked closer at Cherry. Dark grooves circled her eyes. Her skin had a pallid cast, made all the worse by the ugly overhead fluorescent lights. Despite the misery coursing through her, it was all Hailey could do not to go over, wrap her arms around the woman and pull her into a tight hug.

"It's none of my business, but are you okay?"

Hailey waited to be rebuffed. Just because Cherry had just been privy to her personal humiliation didn't make them bosom buddies.

"I feel bad. I didn't realize how much you had on the line with this deal," Cherry said, not looking at Hailey as she ran her hand over the heavy satin of a forties-inspired nightgown.

"My future was riding on it," Hailey said quietly. Not

to add any pressure to the woman, but for crying out loud, maybe it would be nice if people started considering someone else for a change in this little scenario. Rudy was all about self-indulgence. Cherry was totally self-absorbed. And Gage? Hailey ground her teeth together. Well, he was simply greedy and selfish.

So despite her dislike for emotional manipulation, she gave Cherry a direct look. "I have a dozen people who are depending on me, on my business, for their jobs. They have kids, families to support. We've put everything into this, and I really, really think Merry Widow is the best choice for this contract."

Cherry's nod was slow, her sigh deep.

"You're right. It is best." Then, with a loud swallow, she sighed again. "Actually, I've been on the fence, but today pushed me over. I'm not going to do the spokesmodel gig."

Oh, hell.

Hailey wanted to cry.

Or scream.

Screaming would be good.

But she only screamed inside her head. Never outside, where someone might hear her and be upset.

God forbid Hailey upset anyone with her petty personal issues.

But dammit, she'd tried so hard. She'd banked everything on this. She'd truly believed she'd get it, that all she needed was to get Cherry on her side.

And now?

Now it didn't matter. Rudy had already decided on Milano. Without Cherry's vote, he'd simply do what he wanted.

Still, Hailey dropped to a chair, her butt hitting the hard wood surface with a thump.

She was done.

It was over.

"I'm sorry," Cherry murmured, her voice seeming to come from much farther away than just across the room.

Hailey shrugged. She tried to pull out her brave face. Shouldn't be hard, right? She seemed to live in it. But she couldn't. Not this time.

She tried to find some happy words to brush off the whole thing, to make Cherry feel better.

But she couldn't. Not this time.

This time, she really wanted to scream.

On the outside.

"I needed this," she murmured instead. "I knew Rudy would take the sexy sell. That was pretty much a given once Milano got mixed up in the deal. But I needed this."

"You thought I was your answer." Cherry's statement wasn't a question. It was a simple acceptance. "You figured I'd see the merits of your line versus the leather."

"Didn't you?" Hailey lifted her head from her hands to stare through dull eyes.

Cherry nodded. "Yes. Of course I did. Given the scope of the launch and the variety your designs offered, I felt yours would be the much stronger line to feature."

Hailey tried to find some comfort in that.

All her life, she'd searched for the silver lining, holding tight to it when she was being deluged by the cloud. But this time, the lining meant nothing. It could have been pure gold, and it still wouldn't have helped her.

"Why'd you drag this out? Why'd you let Rudy, let me, think you were on board? Why couldn't you have just been honest from the beginning and said you didn't want me?"

Hailey winced as those last words escaped, knowing they weren't Cherry's to own. They were more a summary of every freaking time she'd been screwed over in her life. By her mom, who was always off chasing her dream, running after the next exciting thing and too busy to care about her daughter. By her father, who'd built his

new life and liked to pretend that Hailey was a part of it,
but who never—ever—tried to make her one of the family. By her mentor, who'd sworn he'd file the paperwork
for the business.

And by Gage, who made her feel things she'd only read
about. Who made her hope for more. Hope for everything.
And then who made her think that maybe, just maybe, this
time she'd get it.

"It wasn't fair," Hailey finally said, for the first time in
her life, letting herself express how disappointed she was.

"I thought I could handle it," Cherry said, lifting both
hands in the air. "I thought I could juggle it all."

"Juggle what? Your career obligations? Your love life?
Holiday shopping? What did you need to juggle here? All
you had to do was make a decision, wear some outfits for
a weeklong photo shoot and do one simple fashion show."
Yelling the last word, Hailey realized she was standing
on tiptoe in her attempt to put as much force behind the
words as possible.

Cringing, she immediately dropped back to her heels.

Lovely. She'd just yelled at a very nice, very influential
woman. Good thing her business was ruined. Otherwise
she'd be freaking out in paranoia over the probable outcome of finally letting loose.

"I've been diagnosed with cancer. Breast cancer. Right
before Thanksgiving." Cherry's voice, husky with pain,
was barely audible. The redhead looked down at her fingers, twining them together then pulling them apart, then
starting over again. Her swallow was audible from across
the room, echoed by the sound of the outer door closing.

Gage was gone.

But Hailey could only stare, her heart devastated.

But not for herself.

For the woman sitting in front of her.

"How bad…? I mean, what's the prognosis?"

"It's metastasized." Cherry gave a shaky smile, then gestured to her ample curves. "Looks like these babies are going bye-bye. That's the oncologist's recommendation. I've been fighting it, thinking somehow, if I just believed hard enough, I could change things."

She sniffed, then lifted her shoulder.

"All my life, I beat the odds because I believed I could. I did what everyone said was impossible. My career, my recording contract, moving into the movies and modeling." She looked down at her hands again, then gave Hailey a tremulous smile. "I thought I could believe this away. Silly, huh?"

Oh, God.

"No," Hailey whispered, her throat clogged with tears. "Not silly at all."

This time, Hailey couldn't stop herself. She rushed across the room and took the other woman into her arms. Together, they held tight, tears flowing in an aching river of misery.

Talk about perspective.

14

Gage strode through his father's house, anger propelling his every step.

Damn Hailey for not jumping at his deal.

Damn Rudolph for making it so easy to steal the account away from her.

And damn his father for boxing him in, forcing him into this position. All because the old man had some twisted idea of heritage. A man who, Gage realized with a growl, hadn't ever once decorated a damned Christmas tree with his sons.

He stomped into the lounge, glaring at this year's tree in the corner, then sharing that look with his brother, who was cozied up with his newspaper and a glass of brandy.

"Where's the old man?" he asked, preferring to get it all over at once.

Devon's shrug made it clear Gage's preference wasn't going to matter. "No clue. I think he might have a date."

Both brothers slanted a look at the tree. Decorated in its customary red-and-green balls, it looked like it always did when it was just the three men. Gage was sure their thoughts were in sync. If the old man was on a date, what was the tree going to look like next year?

"Did we ever decorate the tree ourselves?" he heard himself ask. At Devon's puzzled expression, he elaborated,

"I don't remember decorating. I know we always had a tree. But did we have any kind of, you know, tradition or part in it? Or was it always like the wives, simply showing up one day as a big surprise, causing an uproar for its limited time here, then the old man tossing it away when it started to droop."

Devon's smirk faded into a squint as he thought about the question.

"I don't remember decorating. That's a girlie thing, though, so it can go right there with wearing makeup and going to dance class on the list of things we're glad we missed out on."

Girlie. Right. Along with traditions, emotions and anything that couldn't be tracked on a ledger sheet.

"Today was the meeting, right?" Devon asked, as if he were reading Gage's mind. "You nailed down the deets on the Rudolph deal?"

Still staring at the tree, Gage shrugged.

"I've got a new venture I just bought into. Another club, but more S and M focused, less pussycat fluff," Devon said after a minute or so. The silence was obviously bugging him. "You want in? You can take a look at the prospectus, write up a marketing plan, make us both rich."

When Gage's laugh came a second too late, Devon scowled.

"What's the problem?"

"Do you ever get tired of chasing new ventures? Of hopscotching from project to project?"

"I'm at Milano long-term, so everything else is about short-term. That's how you should be looking at your little marketing start-up, too. Get it going, have fun with it, then once it's solid, sell it off." Devon grinned. "Should make for a fun year. And who knows, maybe you'll finally beat my side earnings. Probably not, but you can try."

Rather than incur another scowl, Gage offered up the

expected smile. But he just wasn't into it anymore. The competition, the constant searching for something new, the next big thing. He wanted to settle in, manage his business and see how far he could take it. He wanted to build some traditions, and yes, maybe even learn from a few failures.

He thought of Hailey, of her determination and drive to do everything she could to succeed. He wanted that.

Hell, he wanted *her*.

"What's your problem tonight?" Devon snapped, clearly not happy with the mood Gage had brought into the room. "Did you get the account or didn't you?"

Gage opened his mouth to snap that of course he had. Then he frowned and shrugged instead.

"I want out."

"That's the deal. You get the account, you get out for a year." Devon folded his paper in neat, tidy creases and slapped it against his knee. "The terms were clear."

"I don't care about the terms, or that offer," Gage said, realization dawning. He shoved his hands into his pockets and stared at the tree. Unable to stop himself, even though he knew he was probably cutting his own throat, he repeated, "I want out."

His brother laughed and gave him a derisive look.

"You'd give it all up? Your future? The future of any rug rats you happen to have? Don't you think your kids would someday be a little pissed to find out you threw away their heritage?"

"I'm so freaking sick of hearing about the Milano legacy. We've heard it all our lives and what's it got us? We don't have a heritage. We don't have family memories. We have a despot at the head of the dinner table and the board table, calling the shots on the business and on our lives."

Gage glanced around. "Is this heritage? We've never decorated a tree together. We've never had fun family memories. We're stockholders, assets, prime Milano resources." Gage gestured to the tree, as if it epitomized his every point. "I'd like to think that if I someday have rug rats, as you put it, they'll want more than shares in the company. They'll want holidays and traditions and cookies for Santa. They'll want more than a cold, choking tie with a million conditions on it."

"Money, success, a family name," Devon countered. "Those all buy a hell of a lot of memories and make the holidays a lot more enjoyable. All thanks to those ties you're bitching about."

"Shouldn't ties be deeper than that?" Gage growled, throwing his arms in the air in frustration. "Shouldn't they be more than a fragile thread, easily snapped because I refuse to continue giving up my own goals, my own dreams, to toe the line?"

Shouldn't they be important enough to care that he didn't want to screw over a woman who meant a lot to him, just to snag the company yet another feather for its overstuffed freaking hat?

"Well, that's an interesting take on the traditions I've handed down to you."

Shit. Gage cringed. Even Devon winced as they both shifted their gazes to the doorway.

"Dad. I didn't know you were there."

"Obviously." Marcus crossed the room to pause in front of the tree, inspecting it much as his sons had earlier, then turning to take his favorite seat by the fire. "So you want to break tradition, do you?"

Devon's look was pitying, as though he felt as if he should leave the room so Gage could be shredded in private, but couldn't resist the show. Or, if Gage were in a generous mood, maybe his brother was sticking it out for moral support. The reality was probably propped somewhere in between.

Gage met his father's stare with an unwavering one of

his own. Well, one way or another, Hailey was right. It was time to step up and stand up.

THERE. HAILEY CLAPPED her hands together to indicate a job well done and stepped back from the tree to admire her handiwork. Beads and balls and dainty lace roses, a garland of ribbon and a few scatters of crystals here and there for accent.

The perfect, beautiful tree.

She sighed, letting her smile drop.

She'd rather have the paper snowflake, popcorn and condom-covered one. Of course, she'd rather have it because it came with a very sexy, usually naked man underneath.

And with a promise.

She dropped to the couch, the tree a blur.

"The tree is lovely."

"Thanks." She offered a warm smile to Cherry, who was curled up in the corner chair. The other woman still looked fragile. As if a loud noise would shatter her. But she had an air of peace about her now, too.

Hailey figured that probably had more to do with the ice-cream sundae and Christmas-cookie binge than anything Hailey had done. But if a few hours of listening, another few of hugs and tears and a couple of vats of hot fudge had helped, she was thrilled.

"You're upset about Gage?" Cherry observed after a few minutes of silence.

They'd talked about her cancer, about the holidays, about their favorite junk food and the hottest actors. They'd covered lingerie, a mutual shoe obsession. And now, apparently, they were on guys.

Lovely. But as they'd silently established at the beginning of this bonding session, nothing was off-limits. Hailey knew it wouldn't be fair to sidestep just because she didn't want to talk about Gage yet.

But *upset* was an understatement.

Heartbroken, devastated, miserable. Those came closer.

"Disappointed," Hailey finally said. "But Gage, the lingerie deal, they're minor. Especially compared to what you're facing."

"What I'm going through doesn't mean your pain is any less, you know," Cherry chided, pushing her hand through that luxurious mane of red hair as if appreciating every strand.

"Maybe not, but it definitely puts my heartbreak and business woes into perspective."

Cherry's phone buzzed, the tenth or so time that evening. She looked at it and sighed.

"I've got to go. I have a show at eleven and my car is on its way." Cherry gave her a warm smile, then offered, "This was wonderful, though. And now we have it down pat for our next visit. First I whine, then you whine? We just keep taking turns."

Hailey laughed. Then, remembering the reason she'd brought Cherry back to her place instead of going to the other woman's—besides the ample supply of cookies here—she jumped up and, with a murmured excuse, hurried into the other room. She was back in a quick minute with a gift-wrapped box.

"I intended to give this to you after we'd signed the deal, but, well, that's out the window," she said with a shrug as she handed Cherry the beribboned gift. "It's just a little something I thought would suit you. Go ahead, open it now."

Excitement, and the special joy that came from giving a gift that meant a lot, filled Hailey as Cherry tugged at ribbon, pulled at paper. When the woman opened the box and pulled out the hand-beaded, royal-blue forties-esque nightgown Hailey had designed just for her, it felt fabulous. Even better was the wide-eyed look of amazed appreciation on the redhead's face.

"Oh, this is gorgeous," she breathed. She pulled it close, holding it against her chest as if to assess the fit. Then, with a sniffle, she lifted tear-filled eyes to Hailey's.

"It's cut to drape from the shoulders," Hailey pointed out, having to push the words past the lump in her throat. "It'll flow to the hips, then swirl to the floor. No matter what your size, it'll look amazing."

"It's as if you knew…"

"No," Hailey quickly denied. "It's simply the design. Too often, women are objectified. We're made to feel beautiful only if we fit a specific mold, if we wear a specific size. But beauty, sexuality, that comes from within. Not from what fills our bra."

Hailey sniffed, wishing she had the right words to let Cherry know that she'd always be gorgeous, always be sexually appealing.

So, instead, she shrugged and offered a smile. "It'll be beautiful on you. Always."

"I wish there was something I could do," Cherry murmured, her fingers sliding over the heavy satin, then trailing along the delicate lace. "You're so sweet, and I feel like I just destroyed your world."

"No," Hailey objected quietly. "My designs suit you, suit a woman who wants to feel beautiful, feel feminine. That's not the direction Rudy is going. Even if I'd got the deal, the message would get lost in all the sloppy sex stuff he was going to throw in there. Leather panties, dinosaur shoes. The man has seriously horrible taste."

They shared a grimace.

"You're right. Your designs make women feel great. Sexy and strong." Cherry's words trailed off and she gave Hailey a considering look.

"What?"

"Well, I know you needed the contract. And I have no idea what position your company is in now that you didn't get it. But, and I'm not saying I'm sure of this, but I was just thinking that it might be interesting if we..." Her words trailed off, her gaze intent on the nightie in her hands. After a few seconds and a deep breath, she lifted her eyes to Hailey's. "What if we did a line together? You design. I model. Through all of these pitches, I've loved your message, your passion for how romance and emotion are sexier than lust."

"Launching a line together would mean you're putting yourself, your struggle and your body, on display," Hailey pointed out quietly. She knew Cherry knew that, but it was one of those things that needed to be said out loud. A few times.

"I know. I think this might be what I need, though." The redhead arched an elegant brow at Hailey. "And maybe it can be what you need."

Could it be? Hailey's mind spun in a million directions at once, all of them excited, none of them sure.

"Together?"

"Tentatively," Cherry said, swallowing hard. "I'll be damned if this disease is going to beat me, destroy my confidence or my career. I was going to agree to the Rudolph deal because I wanted exposure."

"Our launching a line together, based on your story, might mean a lot more exposure than you bargained for," Hailey said carefully.

She didn't want to get too hopeful. She definitely didn't want to profit from the other woman's struggles. But oh, the possibilities. The idea of sharing her vision, the concept of expanding people's views of femininity and sexual appeal, it made her want to cry with joy.

Somewhere between a grimace and relief, Cherry checked her buzzing phone.

"My ride is here. I've got to go. Let's both think about this. A couple of days, maybe through next weekend. I don't want to make promises I can't keep. And you need to be sure this is enough to save your company." The redhead rose, her nightie draped over one arm and both hands outstretched to take Hailey's.

"I think this could be incredible," she murmured.

Hailey's mind was spinning. It would be amazing.

But she'd have to step up herself. She'd have to find a way to keep her business, without the Rudolph account.

But if Cherry could face this and find a way, so could she.

"I think it could be, too," Hailey finally said.

With that and one last hug, Cherry smiled and floated out of the room. Hailey grinned. The woman was pure glam, even at her lowest.

As the echo of the shutting door faded, so did Hailey's smile.

She did miss Gage.

His smile and his tight ass. His laugh and his sexy shoulders. His belief in her, his acceptance of her and his outrage on her behalf. Right up until he'd done the exact thing he was so outraged over.

She sniffed.

Still, something good had come of it all.

Optimism paid off.

Sure, things weren't turning out the way she'd expected and held out for. But they were turning out. She should be happy. She should be excited.

She'd stood up for herself.

She'd made a new friend in Cherry.

She'd found a way to save her business, and to empower someone else in the process.

But all she could think of were Gage's words. How he'd forced her to see how much damage she'd caused herself, her life and her business. All because she was always too worried about upsetting someone else instead of standing up for herself.

He was right.

And telling him off when she'd stood up for herself had felt good. Losing him hadn't. But for the first time in her life, she understood that old saying.

If you love something, set it free. If it comes back it's yours. If it doesn't, it never was.

If she was always too afraid to stand up, to take a chance that someone might leave, then did it matter if she had them in her life?

It wasn't until she felt the chill on her chin that she realized she was crying. Hailey blinked fast, wiping her face. Then, knowing she owed it to herself to make the most of the lesson—because she'd be damned if she'd lose the most important guy in her life for nothing—she picked up the phone.

"Mom? Hi. We need to talk."

HAILEY STARED AT the thick expanse of wood, alternating between wanting to turn tail and run, and puzzling over the view.

Was that a wreath hanging there?

It was round.

It was green.

It had a red bow and—she leaned forward and sniffed—it smelled like pine.

Seriously?

Gage had a wreath hanging on his front door?

It was so out of character for a man who until last weekend had never even decorated a Christmas tree, she wasn't sure what to make of it.

Maybe it'd be better if she left, thought about it for a while, then when she figured out what it meant, came back and tried to talk to him then.

Her fingers tightened on the ornately wrapped box in her hands, and, since her heart was racing fast enough to run off by itself, she gave a nod.

Yep, come back later.

She turned to leave.

Her way was blocked by a large male body.

Hailey screamed. The package flew a half foot and her feet almost slipped out from under her. Thankfully this was one of those rare occasions that she was wearing flats instead of heels. Just in case she had to run.

"What the hell are you doing?" she asked, her words a gasp.

"Coming home?" Gage said, his eyes dancing and his grin huge. "What the hell are *you* doing?"

Hailey debated.

Running now, given that it would require doing a dash around him, was a little silly. Still, silly had a lot of appeal compared to putting her heart on the line.

Her eyes eating him up as if it'd been months instead of a few days since they'd seen each other, Hailey almost sighed.

Damn, he was gorgeous.

"I brought you this," she said, holding up the gift. "So here. Merry Christmas."

She shoved it in his hands and, figuring she'd side-stepped silly, started to leave. She'd tell him all the heart-baring stuff later. When he thanked her for the gift, maybe.

"C'mon in."

Hailey winced. But her feet froze and her body, always ready to do his bidding, turned to follow. Oh, man, this was harder than standing up to him had been.

"I didn't have time to wrap yours," he said after helping her off with her coat. The feel of his fingers, lightly brushing her shoulders, burned right through her sweater.

"You got me a present?"

Hailey gave up trying to look calm and casual, dropping to the couch and staring at him in shock.

"You really got me something? But I yelled at you."

Her mother still wasn't talking to her after hearing Hailey's feelings about being dumped at Christmas. *Again.* And her father? He'd apologized all over the place, then blamed it all on her mother. She still hadn't untwisted that.

But Gage acted as if he wasn't mad. More, he acted as though he'd known he'd see her again, and that they'd be in a gift-exchanging kind of place.

It was as though nothing had happened.

Hailey wanted to grab that, to simply let it all slide. Just pretend everything was peachy, that he hadn't hurt her or screwed her over in the Rudolph deal. Act as if she hadn't said mean things and yelled accusations at him.

It'd be so much easier.

All her life, she'd gone the easy emotional route. Smiles were better than frowns, happy times preferable to angry.

But…she wanted more.

She wanted a future with Gage. To give them a chance and see where things went.

And she couldn't do that the same old, easy way.

Then he asked, "Why wouldn't I get you a gift?"

"Because we had an ugly fight."

"So? People fight. Then they make up, right? At least, that's how I've always heard relationships went."

Relationships. They were in a relationship.

Joy, giddy and sweet, rushed through her. She wanted to stop talking now. To skip right over all this soul-searching chitchat and get down to the naked makeup fun.

But they deserved more than that.

Dammit.

Taking a deep breath, Hailey looked at her hands, then met his baffled gaze.

"I don't know. I've only had one ugly fight, and it resulted in a big family rift. After that, I was afraid to fight. I was too worried that I'd lose whatever crumbs I had if I stood up for wanting more. Or that the person would walk away."

His nod was slow and considering, and the look in his eyes intense. As if he were seeing all the way into those little cubbies and closets in her brain, the ones where she hid all her secrets.

"So where does that put us? That you didn't mind losing what we had? Or that you were sure I'd stick around?"

She peered closely at his face, wishing she could see a hint of which he'd prefer she say. Then, since they'd already established that she was all about telling him like it was, she gave a little lift of her hands.

"Because you let me be me. You seemed to appreciate my strengths, my opinions. Me. I never felt like I wasn't important with you. Or that there were conditions on our being together." She swallowed, hard, then took a deep breath. Big admission time. "I wouldn't say I blew up at you for no reason. I really was angry. And hurt. But maybe, sort of, I was pushing because a part of me wondered how fast you'd walk away once I got in your face."

He arched both brows and gave her an assessing look.

"A test?"

Hailey opened her mouth to deny it, then had to close it. Why deny it.

"Maybe. Sorta." She looked at her hands again, wishing she had something to do with all this nervous energy. Like run her fingers over his body, or touch his hair. But both of those actions would probably change the subject. And as much as she wanted to, she'd rather get this out of the way before they got on the subject of being naked.

"You really did offer me a better deal than I was getting from Rudolph. I could have easily taken a ledger of sales like that to the bank and negotiated a loan. Add to it your marketing package, something with such great long-term possibilities? Turning away from it was the worst business decision I could make. I accused you of putting business, your own ambitions, over what we were making together. But I was the one doing that."

Hailey winced when Gage's face creased into a ferocious frown and he looked for a second as if he wanted to hit something. What? He couldn't take an apology?

"You're killing me," he finally said, pushing off the couch to pace the room. "I had these big plans. I spent the last few days putting everything into place, fine-tuning and perfecting things. And you sweep in here with your pretty smile and fancy gift and blow it all."

She shook her head, wondering if all that humility had ruined her hearing.

"What are you talking about?"

"I quit Milano. Not a break, not a sabbatical, not a sanctioned-but-still-contracted reprieve. I quit." He threw his hands in the air, as if tossing aside his heritage, his family and his commitments. But he didn't look upset. Instead, he seemed relieved. Or maybe that was just what she was hoping to see?

"Is that a good thing?" she asked hesitantly.

"It doesn't matter now. I've busted my ass building a pitch, crafting the perfect way to show you how much you mean and how important you are, and you sweep in here and outdo me. Again. Every damned time I think I've got the upper hand, you outmaneuver, outflank and outplay me."

Hailey had to pull her chin off her chest and force her mouth closed. He was ranting, but he didn't seem upset at all. Instead, he sounded proud. As if he was thrilled with her. As if he admired her. As if he really cared.

"Oh" was all she could say.

Then, as much as she didn't want to, Hailey burst into tears.

"HELL." GAGE CRINGED.

Not tears.

Anything but tears.

"Look, that isn't a bad thing. I'm not upset about being outflanked and outmaneuvered. It's like you being on top. I like that, too."

Well, that got a smile, but didn't stop the tears.

Dammit.

Gage pulled in a deep breath. He wanted to kiss the wet tracks off her face. He wanted to distract her with a naughty promise. But he was a man who knew the importance of timing. He had to do this now. Even though it was probably going to get him more tears, he manned up and took both her hands.

"That's one of the things I admire about you," he said, keeping his words low and quiet so she had to quit sobbing to hear him. "You're incredible at what you do. You're passionate about what you believe in. And you're smart. Smart enough to call me on being a jackass. Smart enough to see my fears and push me to get over myself and go for the dream."

She sniffed, her eyes wide and wet but, thank God, not pooled up any longer.

"You think I did all of that? You actually like that I called you on being a jackass?"

"Well, I'm not saying I want it to be my new nickname or anything. But I appreciate that you see me, that you understand me. And that you believe in me."

She smiled. It was a little shaky at the edges, but filled

with so much sweetness that Gage had to smile back. Figuring he deserved a reward for not running like a sissy boy
at the first sign of tears, Gage lifted her hands to his lips,
brushing a kiss over the knuckles of one, then the other.
She was so sweet. So delicious. Then, his eyes locked on
hers, he leaned in and brushed her mouth next.

So soft.

So incredible.

Her sigh was a gentle wash of emotion. Delight and relief, excitement and joy.

All good.

But he wanted her passion.

And he knew how to get it.

Gage shifted his lips, just a bit, and changed the angle.
With a barely there moan, she opened to him, meeting
passion with passion. Desire with desire. And, yes, baby,
tongue with tongue.

He wanted to stay here. It felt good here. Safe. No emotional risk. A part of him figured he'd already risked plenty
this week. His career. His standing with his family. His
heritage.

There was nothing wrong with waiting a little while
before putting everything else on the line.

Then Hailey gave a tiny moan. Her fingers, warm and
gentle, grazed his cheek. Slowly, as if hearing his thoughts
and giving him a chance to decide, she pulled back.

Her lashes fluttered, and then she gazed up at him.
Those huge green eyes were filled with so many emotions. The lust made his already-steel-hard dick happy,
and the delighted joy gave his heart a little buzz. But it
was the trust there, the total faith in him, that made Gage
want to groan.

With happiness. And in frustration.

Because there was no way he could back down when
she was looking at him like that.

"So," he started, pretty sure this was the first time in his life he'd struggled with the right words to sell his point. "I talked to Rudy this morning."

The excitement shifted in her gaze, a frown leaving a tiny crease between her brows.

Nice job, Gage thought. Maybe next he could tell her Santa was fake and that Christmas cookies made women fat. She'd probably look just as happy.

"I wanted to tell him I was off the Milano account. I couldn't throw Milano under the bus, but did suggest he take a hard look at what sexy really was to women, and to men who didn't use *Playboy* to measure their relationships."

Her lips twitched, but the frown didn't fade.

"He's sick of the whole thing. Said he'd rather the models strut down the runway nude than have to worry any more about lingerie." Gage's lips twisted in a rueful smile. "But he said he was going to think about it. That he'd probably be giving you a call."

Gage waited, ready for her to, oh, maybe throw her arms around him. Squeal with excitement. Offer up her undying gratitude and maybe a little love.

Instead, she pulled away and bit her lip before giving him a grimacy sort of look.

"You're so sweet to do that. I really, really appreciate it." So much so that she looked as if she wanted to throw up, he noted. "But I don't think Rudy is going to want to work with me."

Gage knew for sure the guy didn't want to work with either one of them. But that was beside the point.

"Why not?"

"Because I stole his star," she said, watching her fingers twist together for a second before she met his eyes with a gleeful look. "For a lot of reasons, she didn't want to work with Rudy. So Cherry and I are launching a line together."

Gage burst into laughter. Poor Rudy. Looked as though his models were going to have to strut down the runway naked after all.

"What are you going to do about the payoff?" he asked. He'd already talked to his banker, arranged for a loan if she wanted it. He'd figured on wrapping up the payoff in a bright red box, but knew she wouldn't accept it, so the loan was his backup. Just in case she wanted help.

"Well, after chewing into you, I called my mother and told her off for just about everything," Hailey said, sounding proud. "Then, figuring I was on a roll, I called my father and did the same. And then, since I had nothing else to lose, I called Dawn Phillips and told her that revised contract or not, her father and I had an agreement and I'd met it faithfully for three years. That she'd either renegotiate the terms or my attorney would be in contact and we'd settle it in court."

Gage was pretty sure his grin was wide enough to pop his ears off.

"'Atta girl. You kicked ass. I take it everyone stepped up and took responsibility?" About damned time, too.

Hailey shook her head.

"Nope. My mother cried and blamed me for ruining her holiday. My father said he'd take my complaints under consideration and discuss them with my stepmother."

Damn them. Gage was afraid to ask, but figured he'd started this so he didn't have a choice.

"And the Phillips woman?"

"Dawn?" Hailey pursed her lips before giving him a smile that lit the room brighter than the tree they'd decorated. "She agreed to the terms Eric and I had set. After I'd told her how fabulous the business was doing, and how much more money she stood to make if she let the terms play out for another two years, and then I pay fair-market value on the balance due, she saw the wisdom in waiting."

And here he'd thought he'd have to rescue her.

Gage grinned.

Once again, she'd outdone him.

He loved that about her.

"You're amazing," he said with a wondrous smile.

"I couldn't have done it without you. Without you pushing me, showing me that there's more to a relationship than convenience." She swallowed hard enough for him to hear the click, then took a deep breath and met his gaze. Her own eyes were huge. "I think I'm in love with you."

He'd never heard those words.

Ever.

Gage's heart melted. And then, like the Grinch he'd dressed up as once, it seemed to grow huge. So huge he wasn't sure what to do with it.

All he could do was pull her close.

Before his lips met hers, he whispered, "I think I'm in love with you, too."

As they fell into the kiss, the lights of the condom-covered Christmas tree twinkled.

And Gage had to admit, the holidays pretty much rocked.

* * * * *

COMING NEXT MONTH FROM

HARLEQUIN Blaze

Available December 17, 2013

#779 UNFORGETTABLE
Unrated!
Samantha Hunter
After an explosion leaves firefighter Erin Riley with nearly complete amnesia, she has no recollection of her former lover, Bo Myers, the fire investigator on her case. But their strong attraction is something she can't deny....

#780 TEXAS OUTLAWS: JESSE
The Texas Outlaws
Kimberly Raye
Jesse James Chisholm is back in Lost Gun, Texas, and he intends to do whatever it takes to bring out the bad girl in Gracie Stone before she hangs up her wild and wicked ways for good!

#781 STILL SO HOT!
Serena Bell
Dating coach Elisa Henderson is ready for anything when she accompanies her new client to the Caribbean—anything, that is, except her onetime friend and almost lover Brett Jordan. Suddenly it's not just the island temperature heating things up!

#782 MY SECRET FANTASIES
Forbidden Fantasies
Joanne Rock
I was about to realize my two biggest dreams—opening a shop on the coast, and penning a steamy novel. But the sexy owner refused to sell his property to me. And the hero of my book began to resemble him more and more....

YOU CAN FIND MORE INFORMATION ON UPCOMING HARLEQUIN® TITLES, FREE EXCERPTS AND MORE AT WWW.HARLEQUIN.COM.

HBCNM1213

REQUEST YOUR FREE BOOKS!
2 FREE NOVELS PLUS 2 FREE GIFTS!

HARLEQUIN

Blaze®

red-hot reads!

YES! Please send me 2 FREE Harlequin® Blaze™ novels and my 2 FREE gifts (gifts are worth about $10). After receiving them, if I don't wish to receive any more books, I can return the shipping statement marked "cancel." If I don't cancel, I will receive 4 brand-new novels every month and be billed just $4.74 per book in the U.S. or $4.96 per book in Canada. That's a savings of at least 14% off the cover price. It's quite a bargain. Shipping and handling is just 50¢ per book in the U.S. and 75¢ per book in Canada.* I understand that accepting the 2 free books and gifts places me under no obligation to buy anything. I can always return a shipment and cancel at any time. Even if I never buy another book, the two free books and gifts are mine to keep forever.

150/350 HDN F4WC

Name   (PLEASE PRINT)

Address   Apt. #

City   State/Prov.   Zip/Postal Code

Signature (if under 18, a parent or guardian must sign)

Mail to the Harlequin® Reader Service:
IN U.S.A.: P.O. Box 1867, Buffalo, NY 14240-1867
IN CANADA: P.O. Box 609, Fort Erie, Ontario L2A 5X3

Want to try two free books from another line?
Call 1-800-873-8635 or visit www.ReaderService.com.

* Terms and prices subject to change without notice. Prices do not include applicable taxes. Sales tax applicable in N.Y. Canadian residents will be charged applicable taxes. Offer not valid in Quebec. This offer is limited to one order per household. Not valid for current subscribers to Harlequin Blaze books. All orders subject to credit approval. Credit or debit balances in a customer's account(s) may be offset by any other outstanding balance owed by or to the customer. Please allow 4 to 6 weeks for delivery. Offer available while quantities last.

Your Privacy—The Harlequin® Reader Service is committed to protecting your privacy. Our Privacy Policy is available online at www.ReaderService.com or upon request from the Harlequin Reader Service.

We make a portion of our mailing list available to reputable third parties that offer products we believe may interest you. If you prefer that we not exchange your name with third parties, or if you wish to clarify or modify your communication preferences, please visit us at www.ReaderService.com/consumerschoice or write to us at Harlequin Reader Service Preference Service, P.O. Box 9062, Buffalo, NY 14269. Include your complete name and address.

HB13R2

The Wild Wild West

Ever since his father's famous bank robbery, rodeo cowboy Jessè James Chisholm has been the bad boy of Lost Gun, Texas. A rule breaker. A heartbreaker. But he's still haunted by his history, and the only girl who could match his wildness with her own—until she ditched her own bad-girl ways.

But mayor-elect Gracie Jones isn't quite the upstanding role model she projects. She may wear conservative skirts, but Jesse's return has stirred her long-slumbering wild side and a hunger for his rugged cowboy ways—talk about wild Wild West.

Pick up

Texas Outlaws: Jesse

by *Kimberly Raye,*

available January 2014 wherever you buy Harlequin Blaze books.

◇ HARLEQUIN®
™

Blaze®

Red-Hot Reads
www.Harlequin.com

HB79784